LIQUID COURAGE

A MARRIAGE-IN-CRISIS ROMANCE

BRIDGES AND BITTERS
BOOK 2

LAINEY DAVIS

Liquid Courage: A Marriage-in-Crisis Romance

By Lainey Davis
Join my newsletter and never miss a new release!
laineydavis.com

Many thanks to Arwen Davis and Elizabeth Perry for editorial input.
Edited by The Meet Cute Editor, LLC
Cover by Creme Fraiche Design
Thank you for supporting
independent authors!

 Formatted with Vellum

ABOUT THIS BOOK

What happens when happily ever after...isn't?

On paper, I've got it all...an amazing group of friends, a rabid fan base for my romance novels, and a sweetheart of a husband. Except, these days, his heart doesn't seem so sweet. He also doesn't seem to understand my career...or maybe me at all.

Teddy didn't start out as a stuffy suit. It just sort of happened, somewhere between his MBA and his big promotion and our failed attempts at starting a family. From the time we met on the soccer field, Teddy and I have been inseparable. Only Teddy hasn't kicked a goal in a long time and he doesn't really not unhappy.

Maybe all relationships are like house plants, and the leaves all eventually wither up. That's normal, right? I just wish we could find a middle ground...

CONTENT NOTE

I hope it's not too much of a spoiler to tell you this book features infertility and pregnancy.

At the time I wrote this book, Americans like these characters had a choice whether to continue a pregnancy. Effective June 24, 2022, many Americans no longer have that choice. If I were writing this book today, the plot and emotions expressed would be different. The stakes would be different. These characters would have had a different journey, and I think this topic carries new weight. Because our right to bodily autonomy has been revoked, I know reading this story might be difficult for some. Please know that I am fighting for reproductive justice.

PROLOGUE: TEDDY

12 Years Ago

Thwack.

"Heads up!" My teammate Noah's warning comes a second too late and the soccer ball bashes me in the side of the face, nearly knocking me over. That's what I get for staring.

Again.

I can't keep my eyes off the star forward on the women's soccer team. Not even if it means getting beaned in the head by a teammate.

Noah jogs over and claps me on the back. "You all right, man?"

I nod and try to act casual. I knock on my skull. "Hard as wood."

Judah, another teammate, points and laughs. "Preston said wood!" He gestures at his crotch lewdly and the rest of the team chuckles like a bunch of middle schoolers. These guys have always been a lot better than me at goofing around. We're all playing D-I soccer at Pittsburgh U. We all know the meaning of discipline and hard work—wouldn't be here otherwise.

But the rest of my team also seems to know how to switch all that off. Staring at Chloe Evers is the closest I come to relaxing.

I risk another glance up the field to where the women's team is practicing. Chloe knows how to have fun, too. She radiates joy from 100 yards away. Before Noah clocked me in the head, I was enjoying watching her slot a penalty kick in the corner of the goal and then holler in celebration, her toned legs clenched as she leaned back and roared in delight. What I wouldn't give to feel her muscled calves, taste the salty perfection of her skin.

The instant Noah's kick hit me, I was imagining those muscular legs wrapped around my waist, Chloe screaming in pleasure from me and the things I would do to her. I know she'd be fantastic in bed, because she's fantastic at everything.

At least everything I've seen from a distance.

Even in the midst of concentrating on a footwork drill, I can see Chloe smiling. Her soccer skill seems effortless, habitual. I always feel like I need to give 110 percent. I'm here on scholarship, and I have to defend my place on this team so I don't get dropped. I've seen it happen to guys before—they party too hard, their game suffers, and they lose their starting spot to an incoming first-year...like me.

"Just fucking talk to her, Preston." Judah nudges me with his shoulder. "Ask her who she has for Econ or something." He shrugs. "You're a catch."

Later, in the training room while I'm waiting in line for a bag of ice, Noah shoves me. I stumble, my cleats slipping on the polished concrete floor, and I career into Chloe, who braces for impact and catches me before I fall. "Woah, there." Her voice contains a laugh, the lightness of her tone erasing my panic and frustration.

"I'm so sorry," I stammer. I gesture behind me to where Noah grins and gives a thumbs up. "Those guys are assholes."

"No worries." Chloe shifts her duffel bag to her other shoulder and approaches the ice bin. The roll of plastic bags is empty and she stretches to reach a fresh one from on top of the freezer, the box just out of her reach.

She starts to jump in order to reach the box, and I worry she'll slip.

I swallow and extend an arm to help her, my fingers brushing against hers as I hand her the box. I bask in the warmth of her hand against mine, of her smile again as she thanks me for the assist. She fills a bag with ice and turns to hand me the scoop.

"You're Teddy, right?"

I nod, then blush. "Ted."

Chloe's laugh is a warm rush as I reach into the ice bin. "You look more like a Teddy." She tilts her head to the side. "With that fuzzy, curly hair you've got, you're like a teddy bear." Her eyes widen and she shakes her head. "I'm so sorry. I just met you. I shouldn't talk about your appearance like that. I'm totally wiped from practice. Please forget I said that."

I toss the scoop back into the bin of ice and face her. "You can call me anything you want," I blurt before I can analyze the impact of those words. Before I can second-guess myself. Maybe that blow to the head really did mess with my brains. We stand there for a bit, both embarrassed, and when another player shoves me to the side to get to the ice bin, I groan.

"Hey." Chloe places a hand on my arm. Her fingers are chilly from clutching the baggy of ice. "Want to come sit and ice with me?" She walks toward one of the benches and tosses her stuff on the ground, groaning as she pulls off her cleats, peels off one sock, and props the bag of ice on her ankle, which she props on her bag. I follow blindly and mirror her movements, icing my own sore foot.

She looks around the room and then points at my watch. "You got a timer on that thing?"

"Of course." I don't mean for it to sound so harsh, but I am stunned that someone wouldn't know a sports watch had a built-in timer.

"Good." Chloe leans back against the wall and stretches her arms over her head, giving me a peek at an inch of skin on her stomach where her t-shirt rides up. I groan and then adjust my ice bag so she thinks it's related to foot pain.

She grins. "So we've got 20 minutes to fill, Bear. Tell me your life story."

I snort. "I played a lot of soccer; wound up here."

"That's not a life story. That's barely a summary."

"What else is there to tell?" I adjust my ankle again and feel the bag of ice settle in just the right spot. I feel relief seeping through my tendons. I'm too young to make these sorts of noises while I ice, but nobody ever accused me of acting young for my age.

Chloe shakes her head at me like I said something ridiculous. "There's everything else! Like what's your favorite flower, what position do you play, are you an organ donor..." She gestures at me to jump in but I just stare.

"Those questions are really eclectic." My heart races at the nearness of her. I'm hyperaware of the feel of each hair in her ponytail as it brushes against my upper arm when she shrugs in response. I smell both of our sweat from practice and I think I also smell her sunscreen. "Striker," I mutter. "I play striker."

She nods her head. "You seem like someone who likes to create chaos."

I furrow my brow and twist on the bench so I'm facing her. "Not at all. I'm very methodical."

Chloe studies me and I watch as she wiggles her toes. "Maybe you'd be better at sweeper if you're such a strategist."

Leaning back against the wall, I cross my arms over my chest and consider that. I scratch at my chin. I've been on offense my whole life, fighting for a chance to play at all. "I never considered a move to defense. I've just always played offense."

"I play wherever Coach needs someone." Chloe stretches again and I feel the length of her side pressed against mine. Is she sitting this close to me on purpose? She wiggles. "I just love playing soccer."

And then she looks up at me and licks her lips. She grins. "Maybe you'd like it more if you got hit in the head less often."

I flush despite the ice on my ankle. "You saw that, huh?"

Another grin. "You took it like a champ."

I glance across the room and see Noah and Judah lingering by the door. I use my eyebrows to communicate *get the hell out of here* and, mercifully, they receive the message. Noah gives me a salute as they back out the door.

Chloe groans. "I hate icing. But I also love it. You know?" I nod. "Tell me something interesting. I need a distraction from this cold bag."

My own cold bag is starting to sting a little, and I know we must be nearing the end of our twenty minutes. I can't think of a single interesting thing to say, so I close my eyes and blurt, "An acre of soybeans can make over 80,000 crayons."

Chloe makes a huffing laugh sound. "Did you say soybeans? In crayons? How do you know that?"

I shrug. "I grew up on a farm. My parents sell soybeans to a crayon factory."

She whacks me in the arm. "Shut up! That's so interesting. How did they get involved with crayons? Did you color all the time growing up? Do you get to tour the crayon factory?"

Her questions come in rapid fire, like she's interviewing me for a research paper or something. I just shake my head. "I didn't color much, no. Definitely too busy harvesting the beans."

"I want to hear all about this sometime," she says. My watch beeps and Chloe grunts, bending forward to pluck the bag of ice off her ankle. "That's time."

I hesitate, wishing we could sit here all night, even though that obviously would be uncomfortable. Chloe rises to her feet and rotates her hips. I feel a twitch in my crotch as I stare at her, wondering if I should move the ice from my foot to my lap. She bends to pick up the bag of ice and I try not to look down the collar of her t-shirt, which just results in me staring at the curtain of brown hair streaming around her shoulders. I have to choke back the urge to tug it, to wrap it around my fingers and inhale the scent of her shampoo. "Come on, Bear. You're gonna get frostbite."

She nudges my foot with her bare toe before walking slowly to the sink, where she dumps the ice from her bag. I follow slowly, intentionally, focused on each of my micro-movements so I don't embarrass myself further. I wasn't ready to talk to Chloe yet. I would have made some lists, prepared potential topics of conversation, worked through some scenarios.

But here I am, falling into stride beside her, as if she just accepts that I'm part of her walk home. The guys shoved me into her, she caught me staring at her until I got hit in the head, and she's waiting for me by the trash, a smile teasing her lips. I think about how I just told her I like playing offense. I think about how I feel wild and untamed when I'm near her, when I watch her play soccer. I clutch the rim of the sink and steel myself.

Strikers take chances, right? Gotta take shots on goal to score points. I close my eyes.

"Could I get your number? You know, so I can update you on the frostbite situation."

Chloe reaches into the side pocket of her bag, her smile a little wider now. "I thought you'd never get around to asking."

1

CHLOE

Now

I type THE END and sigh, sinking back into my desk chair. I close my eyes, taking a moment to appreciate the feeling of satisfaction at finishing a draft of another book. *I'm an author.* I sometimes feel like I just dreamed this career and have to remind myself it's real.

I look at the clock. Two in the afternoon. I wish for a moment I could call Teddy and gush about this achievement, but I know he has meetings all day. He wouldn't appreciate the interruption. Same with a text message. His phone would bing or vibrate and distract him.

Worse, he'd see it and not respond.

I crack my knuckles and stand up, unsure what to do with myself now that I got these people in my head to be quiet for a minute. The feeling won't last long. In a few hours, I'll think of things I missed, things that I need to change. I'll start worrying about which details I got wrong and which angry historians will fill my inbox with scalding critiques.

By the time one of my books publishes, it feels like another day at the office. Marketing and creating a launch plan, all of that stuff is just gravy. This right here is the real achievement: finishing a draft of the thing. Revisions and conversations with my editor and early readers...those are the fun part. The draft, though. So much work.

I try not to think about the parallels to my work and my marriage, try not to think about the Teddy I fell in love with as the first draft. That would mean the current Teddy is a finished product and that just makes me sad.

"Nope," I say out loud to the empty room. I can't be a wife who thinks of her husband as sad. Not after all we've been through. This is just a rough patch. To prove it to myself, I pick up the phone and fire off a text.

> I finished a draft of my next book!

And then I wait, way too long, for a response that doesn't come.

There are other things I could be doing. Just because there aren't people clambering for my attention doesn't mean my work isn't intense. I run my own business over here. Not only do I research and write the books myself, I publish them on my own, too. I even established an official business for my books last year: Scandal Sheets Press.

"I'm the CEO of Scandal Sheets Press," I mutter, still surprised I'd be the CEO of anything.

I don't love the business aspect of the business. What I really should do is hire a business guy. Or gal. I wonder if my friend Logan can help me with that, but I also worry it's been so long now that I might as well start over. Or something.

Has enough time passed that Teddy should have seen my text?

In an effort to not stare at my phone, I check on my advertising campaigns. I run ads for my books on social media, and it's been so fun figuring out the best way to fine-tune those to get the most clicks. I recently figured out that the people who tend to buy my books also tend to buy Crock-Pots. So now I target people who love slow-cookers and slow-cooker recipes. There's always something new to learn, some new connection I hadn't considered.

Running my own author business is the first thing that really clicked for me. I think it's because all the tasks are so different. I write the books *and* run the ads *and* hire the cover designer. No two days ever look the same. If only my husband appreciated my need to be all over the place. He sees that sort of thing as a lack of focus. Or at least I think he does. We never talk about my work. Not these days.

ONCE I DETERMINE that the ads are all spending the amount of money they should be, I force myself not to check my phone for a response from Teddy. I email my cover designer to let her know I finished a draft. She immediately writes back with a ton of exclamation points and asks if she can read it yet. I smile at that. I know she's just hoping for details that will inform her design process, but I don't show the rough material to just anybody.

I always say showing someone a rough draft of my book is like letting people see me naked.

I frown, then, because nobody has seen me naked in a long time. How long has it been?

I can't decide if it's worthwhile to try to figure that out.

My friends assume I have a blazing hot sex life. It's a fair assumption, since I write steamy historical romance novels. People have made memes about my spicy scenes, sent me messages about how the sexy bits have helped them revitalize their love life with their partner. I'm glad someone is benefitting from my fiction...

EVENTUALLY I CAN'T STAND it anymore and I glance at my phone. The message to Teddy shows as read, but just as I feared, he has not responded. How long would it take him to send a party hat emoji? To give the message a thumbs up? "Asshole," I mutter. And then I bite my lip. I don't want to be angry with him. We've been through a lot together. He's still struggling.

But I'm struggling, too.

I take a deep breath and close my laptop. I neaten the papers on my desk and return my research books to their shelves. I flick off the light in my office, close the door, and walk outside to check the mail. My breath catches when I see the envelope from the insurance company—an invoice. Part of me wants to pay it and shred it immediately, to spare Teddy having to look at the black and white reminder from the fertility clinic. Part of me wants to staple it to his pillow to force him to talk about it with me.

Instead of doing either, I leave the mail in the box and walk away. I need to get away from this house for a bit, enjoy the sunshine. How often do we get sunny days in Pittsburgh? Not nearly enough. I stand in my driveway and remember that I live in the suburbs. My neighborhood doesn't have sidewalks, and there's not really a destination I can reach on foot without crossing a highway.

I touch the keyless entry to the fancy car Teddy bought

me with his last promotion. I climb in the drivers seat and head toward the city, back to the neighborhood where we bought our first house right after college, when we could only afford a fixer-upper and when we worked together to fix it up ourselves. Teddy was so angry when I refused to sell the house in Highland Park, but even he has come to admit it's been a good idea to hang on to it as a rental property.

After all, he's always saying I have plenty of time to manage the tenants. I roll my eyes, trying to remember the last time I took an afternoon to check on the house. I drive over there, wondering why I don't just explain to Teddy that my days are full of data analysis and drafting marketing copy in addition to writing sweeping historical romance novels.

I pull up to the curb outside and smile at the hoard of kids sprinting up the sidewalk from the neighborhood school around the corner. I watch as a sea of dark-haired boys floods into the old Peterson house. I used to babysit for Doug and Amy sometimes when Teddy and I first bought this place. I remember that Amy is a Rogers now, and the Peterson House is technically the Rogers House. Alice Peterson Stag lives just around the corner with her own trio of rowdy boys.

I love knowing the history of this neighborhood. Living here made me a historian—I started researching these beautiful old buildings and learning about the long line of families who lived here. I guess I always imagined starting my own family here. Teddy viewed our house as as a starter house, but I think it was more to me. I should have spoken up about that.

I take a deep breath, noting the neatly mowed grass at our house, the tidy curtains in the windows. I'm about to put the car in gear and head home again when I see my tenants come out the front door. Julian holds the storm door open for Isla as she locks the door and turns to grin at him, a massive pregnant belly jutting before her like the prow of a ship.

Like a beacon or a billboard, shouting that this couple has done it: they've checked all society's boxes. They only signed their lease a few months ago. She must have been newly pregnant, still not showing. I'm glad I didn't have to do paperwork with them when she was visibly pregnant, didn't have to school my face muscles into a supportive, happy expression. Honestly, I still don't even know whether I want to have a baby or whether I wanted to give a baby to Teddy. It definitely seemed to matter more to him.

I try to turn the car back on, realize it's already on, and rev the engine by accident as I pull out from the curb to get away. Hearing the sound, Isla and Julian recognize me and wave. She pats her belly and smiles as he beckons for me to open the window. "You got a second to talk?"

I sigh and turn off the car for real this time, climbing out with a smile on my face. "Place looks great," I say, gesturing.

Isla smiles, rubbing her belly absentmindedly. "I was hoping we could ask a favor." She darts her eyes toward her husband, who scratches at the back of his neck.

I sigh. "Let me guess. You put in an offer on a house?"

Isla rolls her eyes in relief. "Yes. And I'd *really* love to move in before the baby arrives. God, I can't imagine moving with a newborn." She grimaces. "Any chance we can end our lease early? I'll help you find a new tenant!"

I smile, less enthusiastically this time. "Let me talk to Teddy, okay? Text me your closing date and all that."

Julian extends a hand and I hold on as he shakes us both vigorously. "I really appreciate this, Chloe. This wasn't in the plan..."

"These things happen," I tell him, meaning it. "I'm glad you two are on the same page about it." They smile and thank me again profusely as I make my way back to my car.

I check my mirrors for any straggling neighborhood kids and pull out, back toward my suburban upscale life.

2

TEDDY

I STARE at the text from my wife for a long time and I don't know what to say to her. And then I feel like shit because I should know how to respond to a text like that...Chloe took the time to tell me she finished something. She's probably proud of herself, looking for a high five. But what if she's sad that she finished the book? We used to talk after the soccer season about how it's sad to be done. There's grief in endings.

I wish she'd given more context. Or called me so I could pick up on her tone of voice. I should call her. I definitely don't have time for that.

I'm only a month in to my new role as VP at work.

I sigh and run a hand through my hair. I got this opportunity because I presented myself as a stable man, a dedicated employee who was going places...including the country club in the suburbs, with the wife and kids in tow. I clench my jaw thinking about the ways I failed to live up to those expectations. Just another entry on the list of ways I'm not the man I always dreamed I'd be.

I'm still staring at my phone when I hear a rap on my door. "Yep," I say, shoving the phone in my desk drawer.

One of my direct reports, Yvonne, grins and walks into my office. "Ready for our one-to-one?"

I smile back at her and nod, gesturing to the seat across from me. She sits and pulls out her tablet. Yvonne taps a stylus against her brown cheek expectantly and asks, "Where do we stand with the Hopkins contract renewal? My team can start customizing online tools for them, but I don't want to start until I know we have it in the bag."

I grin and lean back in my chair. "Waiting on the courier with the signed documents."

"Courier? Seriously? You know this is a tech company, right? Is this courier riding a clydesdale? Why not just send a fax while you're at it." Realizing what she's said, Yvonne winces, but I laugh.

"You can still bust my balls, Vonnie. I know this promotion is new." I wave a hand. "Legal counsel wanted hard copies. Something about a new tax law for interstate commerce."

She nods. "All right. Sorry I snapped like that. A courier is weird, though. Don't you think?"

I shrug. I tap my touchscreen and pull up the agenda for our meeting and spin the screen so we can both see it. For the next half hour, we review contracts and upcoming opportunities. She is definitely energized by this process. I always seem to feel intimidated by it all, holding my breath like I'm one mistake away from being sent back to the farm.

Holding up her tablet, Yvonne clicks a few buttons on our flagship product page. "And that, Theodore, is called forecasting. Just with data instead of snowfall."

I nod and look out the window at the sky. "You think it'll snow this week like they said?"

She shrugs. "I don't think the weather service uses our software. Maybe they should? What do you think?" By the time she and I ponder the merits of going after the meteorology sector, I'm late for my next appointment.

José, my admin pokes his head in the door, joined by Yvonne's admin and both of us laugh a little. It's good to laugh, ease the tension a little bit. My wife says I get too deep into my own head when I spend too much time alone. I study everyone's wardrobe as they vacate my office. Even as VP, I probably wouldn't have to wear full suits every day. I admit that Yvonne and the others are still doing exemplary work in their business casual attire. But I need the armor of a tailored suit. I spend a lot of time working on this role—I wasn't always a businessman and I didn't grow up in a family where men wore suits to work.

Professional doesn't come naturally to me.

Nothing comes naturally to me. All of it takes hard work and concentration.

Yvonne waves as she walks out of my office. "Give Chloe my love, please. Oh, and tell her congrats on finishing her book. I can't wait to read it!"

I raise a brow. "She told you she finished it?"

Yvonne and her admin both laugh. "Duh, she posted about it on her fan page. God, you must be so excited to find out who Avery's hero is going to be. At the end of *Rebel Heir* it seemed like she could go for Albert *or* Thomas." Yvonne gasps. "You don't think Chloe would have her get with both of them, do you?"

Wide-eyed, I shake my head, not entirely certain what she is talking about. I haven't read Chloe's book. I thought the fiction was just a side hobby for her to use up all the extra tidbits she unearthed in her historical research. She sometimes asks to sit and talk with me about her business, but I haven't made the time.

I kept saying I had to focus on my profile leading up to this promotion...and it stings remembering that she stopped trying to talk about work after our pregnancy plan didn't work out.

Great. Now I feel even more like a failure for letting down my wife.

Yvonne hurries down the hall and I gesture for José to bring in my last appointment of the day. Tonight, I should sit down with Chloe. Hash things out. See what she wanted to tell me about her book.

Tonight, I should bring her a cookie from her favorite bakery, or take her out to dinner. I sigh, realizing it's too late in the day to get a reservation anywhere.

I know that by the time I get home, she'll have dinner made and she'll have a whole list of things to discuss. And I'll swallow the lump in my throat, all the things I don't know how to tell her. We'll sit there and eat asparagus and talk about paint color, and I won't know how to bring up the real things.

The things I don't know how to say.

3

CHLOE

TEDDY HAS his phone out during dinner. His dark eyes turn down toward his screen, his perfectly gelled hair aimed at me instead of his face. I sit there, glaring at him, daintily eating my chicken as he does...whatever it is that he's doing on his phone. Since when do we do this at dinner?

"We're still going to the homecoming events this weekend, right?" He finally looks up from his screen. I guess he's calendaring. I smile and nod. He frowns. "Should we get a hotel room? Probably easier since there's stuff Friday night and Saturday morning, right?"

I nod again. It's hard to believe we're looking at our ten-year college reunion. Both of our college teams have home matches this weekend, as well as social opportunities for alumni. For former D-1 athletes, 'social opportunities' is code for pickup soccer on our old stomping grounds.

"Are there any rooms left near campus? We should probably have looked into that sooner. I sometimes forget we don't live a short bike ride away anymore..." I drift off, hesitant to bring up our old house. Although I did promise Julian and Isla I'd talk to Teddy about their lease.

Teddy clicks around on his phone. "Found us a suite right in Oakland. Although parking will cost more there..."

I roll my eyes at him. "I think we can afford the parking."

He sighs. "True." He forks the last bite of his chicken into his mouth. "We should probably go find our gear, huh?" Raising a brow at me he stands up and walks over to the basement door. I want to ask him if he plans to take his dishes to the sink, but instead I follow him downstairs, to the neat shelves of our old things. From our old lives.

He finds the plastic tub marked ATHLETIC GEAR and stretches up to pull it from the shelf. He's still wearing his dress shirt from work, although his jacket and tie are draped over a chair in the dining room. I bite my lip, wanting to make a comment about him not getting dirty pulling down the dusty boxes. I get like this sometimes, unable to tell him all the thousands of things swirling in my head so I focus on insignificant things just to have something to say. Maybe so he knows I still see him? He'll take his clothes to the dry cleaner regardless. They can handle some dust.

"Aha," Teddy says, grinning, holding up his old cleats. Neither of us has played soccer at all since we moved up here. When we still lived in the city, he'd go find a pickup game every now and then. Now I wouldn't know where to begin looking for a player group. "And here's yours, babe." He holds my faded orange cleats in his other hand. They used to be so vibrant they practically glowed. I loved how they looked on my feet, especially when we played at night under the lights. Teddy smiles at both pairs of shoes. "Maybe we should give them a rinse."

I nod and approach the box. Deflated soccer balls and broken cones are nestled among diving fins and snorkeling gear we haven't used since our honeymoon. It probably all needs to be thrown out at this point. I wrinkle my nose at the smell of the container and reach in, searching for my shin guards. I feel them at the bottom and pull up the firm plastic shells. "Crap," I mutter, noting the spots of mold on the backs. "I can't wear these."

Teddy looks up from where he stands at the utility sink, washing cleats, in his nice clothes. "What's up?" He walks toward me and peers into the bin. He wrinkles his nose. "Oh, gross, no you can't wear those." He squats down beside me and reaches his arm into the bin, fishing around beneath his ski goggles. "Yes!" He pulls out his own shin guards and turns them over. "No mold." He holds them toward me. "You should wear mine, Chlo. You know I'm fast enough to avoid getting kicked." Teddy winks at me and I elbow him in the ribs.

"Cocky." I drop the moldy shin guards on the ground and take the pair Teddy holds out. My hand brushes against his and he smiles. God, I'm still a sucker for his wink and smile. Giving me his shin guards is really thoughtful, too. It's a nice gesture and I feel warmth blooming in my cheeks in response. "Thank you, Bear."

He reaches out a hand like he wants to touch me, but sees the dirt on his fingers and reconsiders. He withdraws his hand and shrugs. "You haven't called me that in a while."

I sigh. "I haven't seen you much." I bite my lip. I don't want to fight with him. But it's true.

He nods his head. "That's fair. It'll be good to spend time together this weekend, right?" He frowns, staring off at the wall behind my head. "How should we handle the logistics tomorrow? If I drive home to get you, it'll take an extra two hours after work. But I hate to deal with two cars in the city all weekend."

I stand up and dust off my hands, fitting the lid back onto the box of gear. I move to lift it back on the shelf, but

Teddy hurries and grabs it, hoisting it up and into place with a soft grunt. "Well," I say, "I could always ride in with you tomorrow morning, leave our bags in your car. I have some research to get done downtown." I shrug. "I could always camp out at the library for the rest of the day until you're ready."

Teddy leans against the shelf and folds his arms, considering. "That's a solid plan. You won't get bored?"

I spit out a laugh, thinking of how much work I need to do on my draft to nudge it closer to publication. "I think I'll be okay." I bite the inside of my cheek, remembering how he didn't respond to my message, how he doesn't seem to know or care how much work it is to write a book. I stand for a few beats, hoping he'll say more. When he doesn't, I stoop to pick up the moldy shin guards and toss them into the trashcan I keep by the dryer, where I usually just empty the lint trap. "Thank you again for sharing your shin guards." I grab both pairs of cleats and tuck everything under my arm as I move to turn off the basement lights.

"Don't mention it," he says, jogging up the steps. He looks over his shoulder at me. "Should we share a suitcase?"

I nod and follow him. After I close the basement door behind me, I notice that he cleared his plate before he went upstairs.

4

TEDDY

I FEEL a little more like shit every time I look at my wife. There's so much to say to her and instead of just ripping off the bandage, I stay silent. She's silent this morning, too, as she does a final check of our suitcase and packs her bag for whatever she's got planned at the County Office Building today.

Still silent, I pick up the bag and carry it downstairs behind her. I used to always joke that I need to walk behind her because I like to watch her ass. She used to look over her shoulder and smile at me, a mischievous little gleam in her eye.

Today she just stares at her phone as she makes her way into the kitchen. I never have to worry about breakfast or packing lunch because the president of our company set up a system where we have a kitchen on site. I eat like a king every day.

I stand by the fridge as Chloe grabs herself a bagel, wishing I could take her with me to work. Chloe raises a brow at me. "You're not eating anything?"

I'm usually gone by the time she comes downstairs in

the mornings. "We get breakfast at work," I remind her, flipping off lights and making sure the thermostat is turned down before we head off.

She nods. "That's right. I forgot your boss has you all kitted out with gourmet meals."

"You should come in with me, grab some quiche before you head downtown."

Chloe frowns and spins her wedding band. I notice she's not wearing her diamond. I guess she doesn't want to cut anyone playing soccer. "I was hoping you'd drop me and *then* go into your office..."

I nod. "Oh, sure." I open the garage door for her and she walks toward her car as I lock the house. "You don't want to take mine?" I tilt my head at the Escalade, spotless and gleaming like usual. Chloe laughs.

"No, babe, I don't want to take that beast. But you can drive my Tesla." She taps the passenger door to unlock it and tosses her bag in the back seat. I heft the suitcase into the tiny hatch and slap the button to open the double garage door. A memory sweeps over me from my childhood, when all I wanted was an automatic garage door opener. I used to think that's what meant you really made it in the world, not having to climb in and out of the car to hoist the door up and down manually. Dad still insists that he comes out ahead in a storm. I don't bother reminding him I'm not looking to leave the house in a blackout. I don't have animals to check on if the power goes out.

I climb in the drivers seat and slide it all the way back. "Tell me what you've got going on at the county place," I say, clicking my seatbelt into place and adjusting the mirrors for my height. My wife isn't exactly pint sized, but I've still got a good eight inches on her.

Chloe tells me how she wants to study some maps of the

city from the late 1700s. "I want to make sure I get the names of the streets right, for that time. See where the docks were. That sort of thing."

"They have all that info downtown?" I arch a brow as I pull out of our neighborhood, headed toward the highway. I realize that I can take the carpool lane today since I have Chloe along. I grin. No stand-still traffic for once.

"Oh, yeah, they've got everything. I can pull wills from the 1500s. Death certificates, court transcripts. It's all public record."

"How do you know how to find all that stuff?"

I glance over at Chloe and see she's frowning at me. "It's literally my job, Teddy. Where do you think I got all the information for the house histories?"

Damn. I fucked up again. "I'm sorry, Chlo. I never stopped to ask you about your research. I guess I thought there was a library or something."

She sighs. "I guess the County building is sort of like a library. This is a huge county, as you know. There's a lot of stuff. A lot."

She stares out the window and I drive in silence, zooming along in the carpool lane and smirking at the line of cars waiting to merge onto route 279 headed toward downtown. I go through the logistics for the weekend in my head again. Men's and women's pickup soccer on the turf in the stadium, then dinner and drinks with the alumni. The current university teams don't play until tomorrow afternoon, so I guess that leaves a lot of time to chill with our old friends.

A thought occurs to me and sours my stomach. I clear my throat. "Hey, Chlo, you're not going to...tell people... about me, right?"

My heart starts to race as she turns her head to stare at me, eyes wide. "Tell them what, exactly?"

"Jesus, Chloe, you know what."

She rolls her eyes. "No, Theodore. I wasn't planning to lead off my reunion tour telling everyone my husband shoots blanks. Happy?"

"No, I'm not fucking happy. Do you have to phrase it that way? God." I smack the steering wheel with the heel of my hand. I hate when she talks about it so coldly, like she's so removed from what's going on. Like it's all on me.

It is all on me. This is my failure. If we were on the soccer field, if I took a swing and missed the goal, I'd say 'my bad' and move on. If I got home from practice too late to bring the farm equipment into the barn and it got rained on, I'd stand tall and take my father's tirade, and we'd move on. I can't seem to move on from this bodily shortcoming.

Chloe doesn't say anything for a long time. I turn onto Grant Street and forget which exact building she's aiming for. "Remind me which intersection you want."

"There's a loading zone spot by the Mr. Rogers statue." She fishes her car keys out of her bag and slaps them in the console.

"Okay, but can you tell me which street that's on?"

She huffs. "This one. Just stop here. I'll get out at the red light."

"I'm not letting you out in the middle of the street. I can drop you at the building. I can do that much." I grit my teeth and look at my wife, who has tears welling up in her eyes. I take a deep breath. "People are going to be talking about their families, about having kids. They're going to ask us."

"I know that, Teddy." Her voice is quiet.

"Well, I'd like us to decide what we'll say. United front and all that."

Chloe's lower lip quivers. The light turns green and I see the bronze statue of America's Dad, smiling down at his shoes. I pop the flashers on and pull up to the curb. Cars honk behind me.

Chloe sniffs. "I was planning to say we're still figuring that out," she says. She doesn't look at me as she climbs out and slams the car door behind her.

5

CHLOE

I KEEP my head down as I go through security at the City County building. I don't want the guards to see my tears. I don't have colleagues, but the people in this building—I see them regularly enough that it feels like they're co-workers.

Someone huffs past me roughly and cuts me off in the line for the metal detector. I've seen this woman before. She spends long days researching property deeds in the archives. Today she's shoving an entire coffeemaker through the x-ray machine, and by the time she and the guards prod it through the conveyor belt, my tears are long dried. The guard makes a face at me, and we share a silent glance at the rude woman who cut me off in line.

I should have said something, especially when the coffeemaker caused a holdup.

Thankfully my shoes don't set off the metal detector today and I hurry through to the Wills and Orphans' Court.

I used to come here for clients. After I got laid off, I started a freelance business researching the history of some older houses in Pittsburgh. I would dig into the public archives, pull up old deeds and newspaper articles and architecture plans and draw up a whole narrative about the homes and the people who lived there.

Now I come here for inspiration for my fiction. I dip into the old documents, simmer in the ways people used language in each era, write down all the tiny details I can find about how things looked and operated. And nothing is more informative than old wills. People's true personalities shine through in petty squabbles and ludicrous estate demands.

Inside the massive archive, I tip my head in greeting to the staff behind the clear partition and make my way to the furthest table I can find, to gather my wits. Something has to give with me and Teddy. I need to talk about our infertility, about what it's meant for us. The longer we keep *not* talking about it, the more explosive we get when it sneaks up and demands acknowledgment.

I don't even know what just happened in the car. Of course it's reasonable to want a plan for how we'll answer questions from people we haven't seen in a few years. But something about the way he brought it up...I just snapped.

I pull up my phone and start to message my friends. We call our group Foof...Fresh Out Of Fucks. I blush a little at the crass name Samantha came up with for our crew of entrepreneurs, engineers, and all around bad-ass women. A few times a month, we meet up for drinks in the back room of our friend Esther's bar, Bridges and Bitters. After the morning I just had I really need to connect with someone who knows how to express feelings.

> Super rough day for me. Anyone free for lunch downtown?

SAM:

> Come to Vinea and eat with me!

I'm on foot today…Teddy drove me.

SAM:

Ah. Let me see if I can get away.

LYRA:

Sorry, Sam, we've got investors on site for an R&D proposal today

SAM:

Shitballs. I'm sorry, Chlo. Can I take you out tonight after work?

I have a thing this weekend. It's okay.

PIPER:

I can do 1230. Want to get meatballs?

ESTHER:

If you come to the bar I can ply you with alcohol while I do inventory. Pipes, get meatballs to go for all 3 of us?

PIPER:

[bacon emoji]

ESTHER:

??

PIPER:

there isn't an emoji for meatballs!

Thanks, friends. I really need this.

I TAKE a few deep breaths and pull out my notebook, finally ready to face my day researching my book. After I get the general draft down on paper, I like to go through wills and marriage records from families living here at the time, to get a feel for what people owned, what they valued enough to mention in their will. The way they spoke about their families in their marriage licenses. It helps me with my dialogue, helps me get in the head of my fictional colonial characters. But then I remember that 18th Century records are kept in a different building.

I groan, but pull out one of the oldest books anyway, heaving the Chloe-sized brick of crumbling red leather onto the desk to see what I can access. I trace my finger along the hand-written index, marveling at the tidy, faded writing. I stop at a random name, Frances Burton, and fill out a request to access his will.

I hand the slip to the creepy guy at the counter, smiling stiffly, hoping my red eyes deter him from complimenting me today. He says my name at least three times as he makes his way into the archives to extract an envelope with Frances's last wishes.

"Here you go, Chloe. Hope you find what you're looking for, Chloe."

I force a smile and slide the file from his hand without making contact.

Frances left $100 to each of his sisters and specified the remainder of his estate—over $1,000, which at the time was an exorbitant sum—was to be put toward his tombstone.

No. Not a tombstone. I squint at the paper. Frances demanded a monument of Rock of Ages Granite.

I shove the paper back in the envelope with a huff. I have no patience for a man more concerned with shipping his monument from New England, no doubt via barge and rail, at ten times the cost he felt his actual descendants should receive. "No wonder you died alone," I mutter, returning Frances's final wishes to the bowels of obscurity deep within the Allegheny County records.

It's obvious my anger with my husband is impacting

even my historical research. I don't really know Frances's story...I'm just letting my imagination assign him the same traits Teddy has, with his calculations and worries about appearance. Our sprawling house might as well be made from Rock of Ages Granite. I return all the books to their rightful places on the shelf and slink out of the room, trying not to make eye contact with the creepy clerk.

It's too early to meet Esther and Piper for lunch, but it's only a mile and a half. If I leave now and walk slowly, I won't be too obnoxiously early to meet my friends. I meander through downtown, imagining what it looked like during the time periods I write about. I realize I'm about to pass the office building where Teddy and I used to work together, where we both got corporate jobs after college graduation.

Now, only Teddy works there. And he thinks I don't have a real job.

While he was on a fast-track to management, I kept getting nudged toward administrative work and I wasn't even upset when I got laid off two years ago. Teddy was, of course. At first.

But then we both decided it was probably a sign: I could get pregnant and spend a year at home with Baby Preston before looking for something new.

I turn right to avoid walking by my former work building, where my husband is now Vice President, and I grin at the sight of the old Union Station building instead.

I snort, remembering it's actually the *new* building. The original depot was burned down during a worker strike in 1877. I snicker, imagining that Frances Burton's monument was lost to the workers' uprising. That would actually work really well as a plot point, so I pull out my notebook and jot that down.

· · ·

BY THE TIME I make it to Bridges and Bitters, I'm not that early. I feel my body relax even more as I peek in the window to see Esther, dancing as she mops the floor. She grins and unlocks the front door to her bar, an elegant renovation of an old building in a neighborhood that transformed from blue-collar industrial hub to trendy center for the arts and food scene.

Esther went for a speakeasy vibe in homage to the area's history with whiskey and prohibition. Everything about this place triggers my interests as a history nerd. That's how I found the ladies of Foof to begin with.

I was on a fact-finding mission for one of my first clients when I wandered into a Foof meeting, admiring the architecture at first and the company thereafter.

I was fascinated by the ways the Foof ladies all encouraged each other to approach their business goals. It was here, at Bridges and Bitters, where I decided to write my first book just for fun. And it was here where I decided to write the sequel, where Samantha squeezed my hand and assured me the royalties weren't going away.

"Hey, Chlo." Esther wraps me in a strong hug and pulls the door shut behind me with a jingle of bells. She nods her head toward a red leather booth. "Have a seat and I'll pull out my latest concoctions." Esther's always working on her drink menu. She only offers a few custom cocktails each month, and they're always amazing.

I hear her rattling bottles around behind the bar just as Piper bursts in the door with a huge paper bag. "I come bearing meat," she yells. Piper slides into the booth beside me. "Sorry if I stink. I had clients all morning."

"Those meat smells overpower whatever sweat you've got going on." Esther sets down a tray with a series of glasses. "Based on your text, I came up with Smoked

Lavender Blues, which is Hendricks gin, ginger liqueur, blueberry juice, lavender bitters, and a squeeze of lemon."

Piper looks at the glass. "What are those floating balls?"

"They're meatballs, Pipe," Esther deadpans as Piper recoils in horror. We both laugh at her and she joins in when she realizes Esther was kidding. "Frozen blueberries instead of ice." Esther shrugs and sits down, rubbing her palms together. "I figure it's early enough in autumn that the blueberries and lavender still count as seasonal."

Piper starts distributing takeout containers from our favorite meatball joint. She's a personal trainer and super into nutrition, so I'm sure we're about to have plain chicken meatballs over brown rice. Even that would have been fine and filling, but I gasp in pleasant surprise when I open my box to find mashed potatoes and gravy alongside my giant serving of beef. Piper pats my leg. "I figured you needed some comfort food," she tells me, digging in to her own predictable healthy lunch.

I press a hand to my chest. "Thank you both for being here for me. I seriously feel better already." I take a sip of my drink and my eyes fly wide. "Esther, this is amazing!"

She grins. "Tell me exactly what you're thinking so I can use your words on the menu."

I close my eyes for a minute. "This is like summer in a glass."

Piper nods. "Late summer and sadness."

Esther squeals and pulls a pen from behind her ear, writing a note on her forearm. She clicks the pen shut and looks over at me. "So spill it, Chlo. What's up?"

I swallow my mashed potatoes and gravy, shaking my head. "It's just...everything. With Teddy."

They both nod and make knowing sounds, like they've

heard all this before. Because they have. "I might have yelled at him about shooting blanks today."

Piper cringes and Esther gnaws on the end of her fork. "Yelled?"

I wave a hand. "He was acting like I was about to air his business to the entire athletic department at our alumni reunion this weekend."

Piper snorts. "Meanwhile you only blab about it to us."

I frown at her. "It's not blabbing with you. I have to talk to *someone* about it. He'd be perfectly happy to pretend nothing's wrong or never mention it ever again."

All three of us take some bites in silence for a bit until Esther says, "I don't know that Teddy is perfectly happy, Chloe. Or happy at all."

I nod as Piper adds, "He seems moderately more happy since he got the promotion, though."

"I guess." We sip and chew a bit more and I finally say, "I wish I could have told Teddy that I was also worried about what people would say and ask. Most of our college teammates have babies...well, elementary aged kids by now. I've seen them grow up on social media." I dab at my mouth with a napkin. "It's going to come up in conversation."

Esther raises a dark brow. "It?"

I sigh. "Babies. Kids. Family planning. The *big it* we never discuss." I take another sip of my drink. "I don't feel comfortable saying something like 'we're both happy with our careers,' because that's not the whole story. And vaginal ultrasounds just aren't good fodder for sideline conversation."

Piper laughs. "That's what you think." She winks at me. Piper has seen and heard it all in her work. She's basically a pelvic floor health expert by now since she trains so many women after they've given birth.

"I'm a terrible judge of what's normal," Esther says. "Bar-tender's curse. Sometimes I think about getting a license to be a therapist. I could bill people's insurance when they come in and squander a stool but never buy a drink."

I smile as the conversation shifts to alternate streams of revenue for both Piper and Esther. I really do feel better just getting a little bit of my frustration off my chest. I don't know why I can't talk like this with Teddy anymore. We used to talk about everything. It's been a long time since he lay with his head in my lap, eyes closed, sharing his secret fears that he'd never live up to his own expectations.

I think about all the things that worried him—that his career would never take off, that his parents' sacrifices to put him through school would have been in vain. It's like he dedicated his life to worrying about the wrong problem. He's finally got the big VP role and the house of his dreams, but we've lost our spark.

And I know it's not just about the infertility. I was miser-able before we learned about that. I just never knew how to bring it up. I shake my head, marveling that I was trying to get pregnant because that seemed easier than explaining to my eager husband that I wasn't sure I was ready to start a family.

After lunch, Piper heads back out to meet another client and Esther says I'm welcome to stay and mooch her wi-fi while she does inventory. I'm not in a head space to write romance today, though. I spend the next few hours mind-lessly counting bottles and kegs with Esther, wondering how I'll face the weekend ahead with my husband.

6

TEDDY

GOD, it feels good to be in this stadium again. How long has it been? I think I was working late the last time Chloe and I came to a soccer reunion, so I missed the pickup game Friday night. Now, even with the stands empty, I feel a sense of belonging and calm as I lace up my cleats. I glance down to the other half of the field where the women are setting up. I grin as Chloe slides on my old shin guards.

This is how we began, with me watching her on this field, afraid to talk to her.

I don't know what happened with us this morning. We barely spoke a word when I picked her up and checked in to the hotel. As soon as we got to the stadium she ran over to greet her old teammates, the group of them squealing and hugging and dancing around.

I'm glad she's happy today. She looks like her old self, smiling, dancing around, wearing shorts despite the chill. Man, I have to stop staring at my wife wearing shorts if I'm going to make it through this game. I finish lacing up my cleats and stand just in time to stop a ball someone sends flying at my kneecaps. I jump backwards to catch the ball with my calf, trapping it with my toe when it lands on the turf.

"Grizz still has it," jokes Noah. He started calling me Grizz sophomore year, when he overheard Chloe call me Bear. Back then I used to play a bit like an angry grizzly bear. The nickname suited me. I felt so hungry then, so desperate to prove myself. I actually used to snarl when I'd go up against another player to try and steal the ball. All the years getting up before dawn to make time for chores *and* soccer practice turned me into a live wire.

The women's alumni sort out colored pinneys to differentiate their two teams, but Noah suggests we play shirts versus skins. It's a bit chilly tonight, but I figure we'll be sweating soon enough. I strip off my shirt and brace myself to get teased. I'm not a division one scholarship athlete anymore, and my body reflects that. Ten years riding a desk have left me a little softer than I used to be, but nobody comments on it. I guess these guys have matured a little since we were in school. It's not like any of them are playing professionally or still have access to professional strength coaches.

"Grizz, you playing up top?" Judah gestures his head toward the center spot. I give a thumbs up and pass the ball back to him, and we're off.

An hour later, we're gasping and sucking down water on the sideline. I almost felt carefree out there. Soccer definitely feels a lot more enjoyable now when I'm not worried about my performance impacting my ability to stay in school. I even laughed a few times when someone kicked a ball right between my legs.

The women are still going strong. It's pretty validating to

see the guys are all moaning as much as me, though. Noah groans as he stretches his hamstrings. "Anyone got ibuprofen? I'm not going to be able to walk tomorrow."

Judah fishes a Costco-sized bottle of Advil from his bag and we pass it around. "My kids warned me this would happen." Judah swallows a handful of the pills. "My four-year-old asked if I will ride the Dinosaur Train to get home."

Most of the guys laugh at that. I know the reference from seeing stuff they post online, but otherwise I have nothing to add as the conversation shifts to comparing our game tonight with t-ball practice or youth soccer. They carry on their discussion while I stretch quietly, hoping this will be the end of the family talk. Maybe I can find a way to slip in a reference to tomorrow's game, or start a betting pool on the score or something.

"What about you, Grizz? You and Chloe ever gonna have kids?"

And there it is. The question I knew was coming.

The question I mentally prepared for. The question I practiced answering until I felt like I could pull off an aloof answer. My guts clench up and my heart races. Sweat pools on my lower back as I think about everything that goes with that question. I swallow. "We're still figuring all that out," I say, stuttering over the practiced line.

In my vision for how this conversation would go, the guys all accept that line and move on. I have no follow-up prepared, so I nearly pass out when Judah says, "Clock's ticking, though, Grizz. At this rate you'll be an old man when your kid goes to college."

I stare at him, blinking. My mouth dries up as I open and close it fruitlessly. I know my teammate shouldn't be saying such things, just as I know people say such things all the damn time. It's the way conversations go for married people in their 30s. *You guys gonna have kids* or some variation of that is a common refrain we hear from the dentist, our mailman, you name it. When it's a stranger or a casual acquaintance, I usually wink and shoot finger guns and say, "I practice every night" or something.

But these are guys who held my hand when we lost a national championship playoff game. These are guys I helped brush their teeth when they had shoulder surgery and couldn't move their arms. I sigh as the silence stretches on too long. "You know how it is, Jude." I shrug. "Chloe might need a little science support for this one."

He nods and I feel like a traitor. Like a filthy liar. Somehow worse than admitting I'm a biological failure...I lied and made them all think it's Chloe whose body refuses to do its basic human functions to perpetuate the species. Noah claps me on the back. "That sucks, man." The other guys grunt in agreement.

I rise to my feet slowly, muscles screaming at me. I pull my shirt over my head and look up to see Chloe smiling as she takes a drink break. She waves, and I nod my head at her, feeling ashamed. I huff. "We going to the bar or what?"

"Where do we even go?" Judah asks. "Panther Hollow Inn closed down right after we graduated."

"Seriously? Shit." The conversation mercifully shifts as the guys pull out their phones and look for a bar where we can relive the glory days, back when our bodies were in perfect physical condition, even if we didn't know we had secret, lurking failures.

7

CHLOE

I FLOP down on the turf, exhausted after we finish our pickup game. "I can't believe I used to do this every day. And on a full field!" Lucy Nelson-Moyer, one of my old roommates, flops down next to me, but she's barely breathing heavy. And she's largely pregnant. "How are you so happy right now," I ask her, shaking my head.

She pats her stomach. "I've got a lot to be happy about! Plus I still play regularly. Hey, you should join us."

I brush my sweaty hair out of my face and ponder this. Earlier, as we were warming up, Lucy mentioned that she still lives in the city. Then I of course felt bad that we hadn't kept in touch. "What's the deal with your team? Teddy and I moved up near Cranberry..."

Lucy groans. "Hm that would be kind of a haul. I'll text you the info about the Phe-Moms, though. It's an all women's team. Everyone's over 30."

"Phe-*Moms*? Everyone's a mom?" My heart sinks. The last thing I need right now is to infiltrate an environment geared around motherhood. I just can't handle it. Not until Teddy and I sort things out. I pay half attention while Lucy indicates that not *everyone* on the team is a mother, but I get the sense that there are often kids around.

Before long, our old captain announces that we are off to join our male counterparts at Fuel and Fuddle. Evidently the guys have taken over the basement room of the bar and ordered a massive quantity of sweet potato fries. My mouth waters at the mention of food and I quickly scoop up my things, ready to walk down the hill to the bar.

"I'm probably going to head out," Lucy says, rising to her feet with a groan. In college, everyone would have pressured her to stick with us. But now, we all just hug our pregnant friend and agree to save her a seat at tomorrow's match. She makes her way toward her car, waving.

The familiar smell of Fuel and Fuddle slams into me when I walk through the door, the floor sticky as ever. I get flashbacks of drinking here in the off season, Teddy's arm slung around my shoulders, his hand tracing the muscles of my thigh when we sat. I've always loved Teddy's thighs...firm and hairy. Soccer players have the best thighs. You'll never convince me otherwise.

I shake my head as we approach the stairs to the basement, where I spy Teddy saving a seat at one of the tables along the wall. His thighs are covered in sweatpants, unfortunately. He grins when he sees me, the first time I've seen him smile in a long time. I drop into the chair at his side as the rest of the women's alumni mingle and merge with the men's alumni.

Teddy drops a kiss on my temple and I turn to stare at him. This is the first we've touched in weeks and the reality of that hits home as I lift my fingers to the space where his lips dotted my skin. His cheeks flush, seeing my movement. "I ordered you a burger," he says, looking at me hopefully.

"Thank you." I smile and reach for his water glass. Always the responsible one, Teddy has a glass of water along with his beer, alternating sips. Even in college, even in the off season, Teddy was a reserved drinker. I don't know that I ever saw him lose control, not to alcohol, not to temper, not to anything. Teddy has always had too much on the line, always been so desperate to rise above his background.

I remember feeling dazzled by his passion, by the direction he knew his life should take. He still thinks his life should take the same direction, while I'm just beginning to figure out what I want.

Judah, one of Teddy's old teammates, does a double take when he notices me at the table. "Holy shit, Chloe, you look exactly the same!"

"Thanks, I guess?"

Judah shakes his head. "It was a total compliment. I wasn't sure if you and Grizz would have just let go, what with being old married people and all."

I squint at his hand. "Don't I see a wedding band on your hand, Judah?"

He cackles. "Yeah. Can you believe I found someone to put up with my shit?" He pulls out his phone. "This is the fam. God love 'em."

I feel Teddy stiffen at my side as we look down at the picture of Judah and his wife and kids. Predictably, the conversation at the table shifts to family life. Even the lesbians from my team have all had babies. I listen, fascinated, as Jenny shares her story about driving through the Fort Pitt Tunnel with a tank of sperm buckled into her passenger seat. I laugh with everyone as she talks about how anxious she was, seeing all the hazardous material warnings posted in and around the tunnel. "Imagine if I'd been rear ended? And sperm exploded all over the tunnel?"

Well, not everyone is laughing. I look up to see Teddy grasping his beer, his jaw ticking as he seems to grit his teeth. I reach under the table and squeeze his leg. He meets my eye and I smile at him. This silent communication is the longest conversation we've had about our infertility. I feel breathless, a surge of longing. I wish he'd hug me or something.

The server interrupts Jenny's story, delivering a tray of drinks and burgers. I practically inhale my food, forgetting how deep the hunger can permeate after a hard workout. Undeterred by hunger, Judah leans forward to ask, "So you just knocked up your wife at home? With the tank?"

Jenny nods. "First time, too." Judah holds up a fist and Jenny pounds it before downing her beer.

Another teammate, Dana, winces. "Yeah, we went ahead and let the doctor handle that part." She shakes her head. "I don't think Linda would appreciate me fumbling around her womb like that."

The table bursts into noisy conversation about pregnancy. From what I hear, the hetero folks all conceived the traditional way...the way Teddy and I can't. I close my eyes and squeeze Teddy's leg a little harder. When I open my eyes, Dana is leaning forward toward me. "Chloe, I heard a rumor about you." My eyes bulge as I worry she can read my thoughts, or that someone had blabbed about our infertility. I nearly choke on my drink. But Jenny laughs. "I heard you write dirty books under a secret name!"

Teddy pounds me on the back as I cough. Once I gain control of my throat I nod. "It's true. I write romance."

Noah frowns. "Grizz, I thought you said your wife is a historian."

Teddy looks at me like I just killed his pet worm. I frown. Is he ashamed of my career or just pissed that he's being contradicted? I turn back to Noah and clarify, "I was writing house histories. That's what got me interested in romance, actually. All those scandalous stories about jilted brides and relationships between the elite and their household staff...I decided to try my hand at fiction." I shrug. "It's working out well."

Jenny pulls out her phone. "What's your author name? Lauren and I read those bodice rippers." Noah laughs and Jenny elbows him. "What? They're good."

I lick my lips and glance at Teddy. He's staring off into the distance. I sigh. "It's Chloe Petals." I clench, waiting for our friends to tease me about the name. "I wanted something that would stand out, but that people could spell. Plus my books feature a lot of flowers..."

My words are drowned out as Jenny slams down her phone. "Holy shit, that's you? Chloe Petals is you? Fucking hell, Chlo. You're not just an author. You're a damned rock star."

Noah and Judah look surprised. Jenny pulls her backpack out from under the table and digs out a tattered copy of my first book, *The Red Coat.* "You have to sign this for me. I've read this a million times!"

"You actually have one of Chloe's books in your bag? Let me see that." Judah reaches for the book and Jenny clutches it tightly against her chest.

"Get your own, man. This one's mine. God, Chloe, when you wrote about the women who made the saltpeter for the gunpowder mill...Lauren and I always say if we were alive back then, that's what we'd be doing. Making gunpowder for the war effort. Wearing pants. Daring men to come fuck with us on our explosive property..."

I smile and reach for the book. "I'm so glad you like it."

Jenny hands me a pen from her bag. "Like it? We have it on audio, too. That narrator's voice is sexy as hell. I say that as a lesbian." I laugh as Teddy, Noah, and Judah continue to stare in disbelief. I hand Jenny back her signed book. "When's the third one coming out, Chloe? *Rebel Heir* was just as good as this one."

I bite my lip and raise my glass. "As a matter of fact, I just finished the first draft of the new book this week."

"Hey, that's amazing. You wrote three books?" Noah looks impressed.

Jenny snorts. "She's on all kinds of best-seller lists. Chloe, you have an end-cap at the library!"

Noah's eyes widen. "I swear, Grizz said you were just writing as a hobby."

Teddy swallows. "It's hard to keep track when Chloe's doing so much," he mutters. Nobody seems to have a response to that. We nibble our fries in silence until someone from a neighboring table suggests we sing the college fight song. After a few rounds, I decide I've had enough reminiscing for one night.

"I'm going to head up to the hotel," I say, standing up and reaching for my bag. I wait for Teddy to join me, to walk with me at least.

"I'll be back in a bit," he says to the guys, but he tosses cash on the table and follows me.

I FEEL his hand on the small of my back as we climb the stairs and exit the bar. The street is deserted at this hour, but the hotel is just a few blocks away and the city is well-lit. So

I'm surprised when he tugs me into an alley and presses me up against a wall. I squeak.

"People know who you are," he whispers, tracing his hand down my cheek, an awed expression on his face. "Women carry your books in their workout bags."

I nod my head, my heart pounding in my chest. Is Teddy turned on by my notoriety? The thought of him being proud of me, of my work giving him pants-feelings sends a flutter of nerves sparking through my belly. "When did that happen?" His mouth is close to my ear, his breath hot on my skin.

I shrug and then shiver, the cold brick seeping through my shirt. At first I didn't want to bring up the books. They were just something to do, something fun. I never expected anyone to buy them, but the Foof ladies encouraged me to publish. I don't have an answer for why I didn't mention my success. It never occurred to me that he would approve of something as risky as "author" as a career.

Then my husband is kissing me, moaning against my neck, pressing against me in the alley.He presses against me, hard and warm, wanting. "Teddy!" I gasp, his name a question and a shout, startling him. His eyes widen and he looks around, tugging me up the hill toward the hotel.

We don't speak as we hurry along the road, jay walking and bursting into the hotel lobby. "Do you have your key?" He starts patting his pockets as I fish the key card from the side of my duffel bag. He yanks it from my hand and uses it to call the elevator. Once we're in the car, he's kissing me again, both hands holding my face, like he's desperate for me.

And I'm desperate for him to want me like this. I moan and sink against him, feeling my nipples harden in a way that has nothing to do with the chill autumn air outside. We tumble into the hotel room and he kicks the door shut behind him, stripping off his t-shirt and backing me against the bed. "You taste sweaty," he pants.

I nod. "You taste like French fries." We giggle as his rough hands yank at my shorts. My thighs are taut and cold from being exposed, the heat generated in the soccer game long gone. I kick off my underwear and shorts together as Teddy slides down his sweats and then kneels above me, eyes wild.

This all feels fast and desperate, but I try to remember that it's been awhile. We probably just need to break the seal, come together and then our bodies can reunite. I suck in a breath as Teddy's cold finger explores my folds.

"Is that okay?" He kisses the corner of my mouth and I nod, relaxing as he swirls and stretches me. I think about how good it always feels when he slides inside me, how much I love just being filled by my husband, pulling him into me like we are truly connected.

He pushes up onto his forearms and looks at me. "What's wrong?" The hard tip of his cock is right there, so close. Why won't he slide inside me? I arch up, trying to draw him in, when I feel wetness on my cheek.

I'm crying.

"Oh," I say, as Teddy pants above me. "It's just been so long..."

I feel the energy fizzle out and I know it's not going to happen. Teddy nods and rolls off of me, lying on his back and staring at the dark ceiling.

8

TEDDY

My neck hurts. I didn't want to wake Chloe when I couldn't fall asleep at 2am, so I watched *Law and Order* reruns on the tiny hotel couch in the sitting area until I passed out. And now we're standing throughout the women's soccer match to cheer for the home team. I groan as I turn my head to glance at my wife, decked out in a tight Pittsburgh U tee. With her hair in braided pigtails, she looks youthful and happy, bumping shoulders with her former teammate Lucy whenever the team does something exciting on the field.

I wish I could bottle up this happy energy, take it home with us. Take it back into that hotel room at least. What in the hell happened last night—my wife cried during sex? She seemed so into it. Until she wasn't.

I wish I could have a conversation with her, but every time I try, I end up yelling or saying something shitty. No wonder we couldn't seal the deal last night in bed. I groan again as Judah leans on my shoulder from behind. "The team really upped their level of skill since we were here," he yells above the pep band. "Did you see that corner kick? She bent it perfectly."

The stadium horn signals halftime and, mercifully, the fans all sit until the action resumes. I try to crack my back, twisting to the right and left as Chloe looks on in concern. She doesn't say anything, though. But Judah does. Fucking Judah.

"Hey, guys, I wanted to apologize for going on and on about babies last night." He claps a hand on my shoulder and one on Chloe's. "That must be rough if you guys are trying and...yeah. Sorry."

Chloe licks her lips and stares ahead, but I sense her stiffening beside me. She can't possibly know I veered from our "we're still figuring things out" tagline. I pat Judah's hand. "Don't worry about it, Jude. I'm glad you're excited about your family."

But then he keeps on going.

"I wanted to let you know my wife's sister is a fertility doc. You know, if you need a referral or anything." Chloe turns to him and then stares at me, eyes wide. Judah continues before I can stop him. "Brooke says for lots of women they just need a special hormone or something and then—" He snaps his fingers and shrugs. "Anyway just shoot me a text. Happy to connect you, Chlo."

She doesn't say anything, just breathes slowly through her nose in a way that has her nostrils contracting tightly with each inhale. Finally, she looks at Judah. "I wasn't aware Teddy discussed our family planning in such detail."

He waves a hand. "Oh, he was super vague. Just said you need a boost from some science." Judah shrugs. "I need some science soon myself to *stop* the baby batter." Judah pantomimes a pair of scissors and then points at his crotch.

Chloe turns white. "I need some science?" She whispers this, aimed at me. I stare at her, ashamed, and swallow. "Give me my car keys," she says, holding out her hand. I nod and reach into my jeans pocket. Without another word, she takes them and storms out of the stadium.

I blow out a deep breath and turn around to face Judah. "I wish you hadn't brought that up, man." He grimaces. "I gotta go after her." I head up the bleacher steps toward the exit just as the fans pour back in for the second half of the game. Ducking and weaving around people laden with pretzels and nachos, I have to sprint to catch up with Chloe once she hits the turnstile to exit. "Chloe!" She doesn't stop. Doesn't turn around. "Babe, can you wait a minute?"

"No, Teddy, I cannot." She says this without turning to face me. "I'd prefer if you find your own way home." I chase her down the sidewalk as she makes her way toward her Tesla.

"Chloe, I'm sorry I told them that, okay? They were just all pressing me about it. When were we going to start trying, how we better not wait too long..." I close my eyes. I know what I did is unforgivable. Hell, I caused a riff yesterday when I pre-accused *her* of blabbing to the women's team about our problems. About my problem. And here I'm the asshole fucking everything up.

She shakes her head and stabs at the door handle, and yanks it open before sliding in and slamming it shut in my face. I can tell she's wishing she could rev an engine or squeal away to show her rage. Instead she navigates the car slowly, silently, carefully out of the parking spot and flashes me the bird as she drives toward our house.

"Shit!" I sink to the curb and tug on my hair. My entire life is falling apart, just as I'm supposed to be reaching my peak. I did everything fucking right. I worked hard in school. I graduated with no debt thanks to my athletic efforts and my parents got to see their son walk the stage, the first Preston to graduate from college. I'm the vice fucking president at my company. I have an MBA from Wharton for Christ's sake, but none of it matters because I can't do the one thing men have been doing since the dawn of the species.

If I can't even knock up my wife, can't pass on this legacy...what does any of it matter? No fucking wonder Chloe is pulling away from me, starting a secret life as a famous author and shutting me out of it. I let out a scream, hoping anyone passing by will think it's related to the game in the stadium.

I pull out my phone and call for an Uber, but when I get home, my house is locked and empty. There's no note and no Chloe. I don't even know if she came here or just took off for...somewhere. I call her phone. It goes straight to voice-mail. I call it again, hoping she's just got Do Not Disturb turned on while she's driving or something, but the call goes to voicemail again.

It would seem I've finally done it. I've driven away the best thing to ever happen to me.

HOURS LATER, there's still no sign of Chloe. I've practically paced a hole in the rug in the front hall, staring at it and remembering how much Chloe didn't even want to move to a house big enough for a front hall. She said all this was showy, and she's right. But I wanted showy. I had to have the perfect house to show the world this amazing woman who somehow agreed to marry me. Me!

I think about how hard I always worked to be moving forward, how much I loved that Chloe was goal-oriented, too. I puff out a laugh and drag my hands down my cheeks. She and I used to communicate about goals a lot more. I stop in front of the hall mirror and stare at myself. I'm no longer as certain Chloe and I even have the shared goal we talked about a few years ago.

Finish my MBA, get a promotion, have a baby...that was our five-year plan when Chloe lost her job. She seemed on board, even seemed to enjoy the house histories she was doing. I'm not sure what the hell happened to that. The house histories were supposed to be part-time, something she could stop once she got pregnant.

So much for that plan, I mutter.

I pace out another few laps as the hall starts to get dark in the fading daylight before I accept that she's not coming home any time soon. I aim toward the kitchen, realizing I haven't eaten since this morning, but then I see the door to Chloe's office is open. I step inside and inhale, the scent of my wife filling the space. The shelves teem with books but the desk is neat and tidy. She uses one of those yoga balls instead of an office chair, and when I notice it I feel another twinge of shame remembering how a friend bought her the ball to use in pregnancy.

She's got the ball propped up on rollers, like one of those little scooters mechanics use to slide under a car. I nudge it with my toe, surprised and impressed that it doesn't fly across the rug. I sit down, hesitantly, and run a hand along Chloe's keyboard. This is the room where my wife spends her long days, and I never bother to ask her about them. She's got a series of sticky notes along the sides of her monitor, with her neat handwriting declaring odd phrases like "scurvy??" and "latrines."

Frowning, I peer into a cardboard box on the desk, which Chloe has used a black marker to label with SIGNED PAPERBACKS. Inside, I see neat stacks of books showing a sweaty man with a ponytail in a passionate embrace with a woman in a ripped dress. "The Redcoat by Chloe Petals," I murmur, frowning deeper. Petals? I have a vague memory of her saying she didn't want to use our last name on her book, to keep some anonymity.

I've never read my wife's book. I chew on my lip, remembering that I never even commented the other day when she told me she finished another one. Glancing up at the shelf, I see that she's published two books...two that she's got displayed anyway. Are there more?

I know the book is a romance. I probably wrote it off initially as *not my cup of tea*. Chloe knows I usually only read nonfiction. If she wrote a biography of Linden Johnson I'd be all over it...

I adjust my weight on the ball and thumb open the book to a random passage toward the middle. My eyes drift to the top of the page.

Sally gasped as her new husband unfastened his sword belt, which hit the floor of their room with a thud. The sound seemed to reverberate along with her racing heart as she stared for the first time at the evidence of Linus McClinton's arousal.

"What the fuck?" I look over my shoulder as if I'll be caught. By whom I could not say. I turn to the next page in the book to see if I've lost my mind, but it's more of the same.

Sally's thighs were warm and soft, in contrast to the corded muscles of her soldier. He settled himself between her quivering legs, his fingers tracing a river of sparks as they sought her wet heat.

I swallow, adjusting my posture as I realize I'm fully aroused by this book. I drop a hand to my crotch, disbelieving until I feel the bulge with my own fingers. I gasp at the contact.

I read the rest of the chapter, not stopping until Linus releases his final, heaving spurt. I'm experiencing a lot of emotions at once. Disbelief, shock, awe...but above all, arousal. My dick is throbbing and I'm sweating with the effort to not pull it out and touch myself right here in Chloe's office. It's difficult for me not to close my eyes and imagine my wife and me in that scene, in the breathy moans she describes on the page.

It definitely wouldn't take long for me to get myself off, not after last night. Not when it's been so long.

I thumb back to the start of the scene and I'm about to reach inside my jeans and relieve myself when I hear someone in the house.

Footsteps approach the office as I clamber to my feet. "What are you doing in here?" Chloe stands in the door to her office with her hands on her hips. Her face is red and puffy like she's been crying. I drop the book and stand, wanting to slam her against the wall and kiss her.

But then I remember.

The fight. The long silences. Me.

She doesn't want me to ravage her. From the look of things, she doesn't want anything to do with me at all.

9

CHLOE

FIVE HOURS AGO...

FOOF CHAT

SOS. I need you guys.

SAM:

Oh my god, are you safe?

PIPER:

Please tell us you're okay.

I'm safe. Awful fight with Teddy. I don't want to be at our house.

ESTHER:

Oh, Chloe, you want to stop by the bar and grab my house keys? My couch is your couch, etc.

PIPER:

I've got a whole guest room, Chloe. No need for a couch. I'll be home in about an hour if you want to come?

SAM:

I'll stop by with fortification.

ESTHER:

We close at four today but I can come as
soon as I wrap up brunchy booze.

> Thanks, Pipe. And thank you all for being
> here. This really sucks.

As soon as I'm settled on Piper's couch with blankets
and a bowl of white cheddar popcorn, with my friends gath-
ered around me for support, I start sobbing.

Piper squeezes my leg. "Honey, you don't have to tell us if
you don't want to."

"Fuck that. What did he do?" Samantha dunks a hand
into the popcorn bowl and crams snacks into her mouth,
waiting for me to spill my guts.

Esther arches a brow. "Is this about baby stuff? House
stuff? You never tell us much personal business, Chlo."

I take a deep breath and a fortifying bite of the popcorn.
"We tried for a year, you know. After I got laid off?

Piper counts on her fingers. "You got laid off like 18
months ago. While Teddy was finishing grad school?"

I nod. "The layoff seemed like a sign from the universe. I
could focus on yoga and eating healthy and get myself all
knocked up while Teddy finished his MBA..." I sigh. "It was
going to be perfect." I meet Samantha's eye. "I was going to
wait until I was pregnant to make a plan for going back to
work after the baby, or see if maybe I wanted to stay home
with the little guy." A sob knots in my throat at the thought
of my imaginary baby. I don't tell my friends that I was more
excited about having a plan than I was about the actual idea
of motherhood.

How do I tell them my period sometimes felt like a relief,
if I was in the thick of a deadline for a client or for my own
fiction? What do I do about that shameful thought now that

we know Teddy and I could never have conceived? It's all so much.

"That must have been really difficult," Piper soothes. "How long ago was that?"

I try to remember exactly when the sex switched from sexy to frenzied, when my periods became stressful, when I started to wonder what life would look like if we never had a baby after all. Conceiving definitely shifted into goal, and I'm still enough of a competitive athlete that I can't turn away from an unmet goal. I shake my head. "I'm not even sure at this point. Eventually I told my doctor we'd been trying and that nothing seemed to be working. They blew me off at first, but I said it really had been a year." I shove the popcorn bowl away. "By that point I was drinking gallons of special tea, avoiding all alcohol, chugging fish oils and things...it was so gross. I thought maybe it was me."

Sam gasps. "It wasn't you?" Esther smacks her and shakes her head admonishingly.

Piper hands me a tissue and after I blow my nose, I explain how we finally got a referral to a fertility clinic. "They bring you both in, and I got sent off for bloodwork and a full pelvic exam while Teddy..." I wave my hand suggestively.

Samantha leans forward on her elbows. "Into a cup?"

I nod. "Then we waited in agony for them to have all the results and schedule us both to come back together. Just doing that was a nightmare with Teddy's schedule. I'm sure he was in denial. I want to say it was a month before we got back in there to talk with the doctor."

I was so sure they were going to tell me there was something wrong with my ovaries, or that the Ph balance in my cervix was rejecting Teddy's sperm. I remember him squeezing my hand reassuringly, like he, too, thought it was my body causing a hurdle.

I hold out my hands, palms up. "They said Teddy's sample had low motility, low numbers. He gave them a repeat sample to be sure."

"Then what?" Piper breathes the question. The room is so quiet and still. I can understand my friends' surprise, since I'd never talked about this issue before. At the Foof meeting soon after, I remember telling them *we* had a setback in our family plans. I always say we. Because Teddy and I are a team...at least I always thought we were.

"Then nothing," I tell them. "He just shut down completely. Won't see the urologist. Won't talk about it. I've been living with his shame and disappointment ever since." I tell them about the cold silence, how we're more like roommates than sweethearts, except when we explosively fight about unrelated issues and then don't talk for a few days before slipping back into our routine of cordial companionship.

"The fertility doctor said there are lots of options, things to try. Lord knows we can afford it financially." I recently decided I hate Teddy's new position at work and the amount of time he devotes to his job. The high salary isn't worth the cost to our relationship. But I don't see him frequently enough to even have that conversation with him.

Esther slides a glass of water along the coffee table toward me. "What happened this weekend? I thought you two were at some alumni thing for soccer."

I take a sip of water and nod my head. "Yeah, and Teddy apparently told the whole men's team that *I* am the one having issues. One of the guys actually offered to connect me with a specialist during the game today. In front of everyone!" My friends gasp and I feel warmed by their indignation. It's nice to be in a place where I'm being supported, where I feel like someone cares what I have to say. I vent about the game until I feel much calmer about all of it.

"I just don't know what comes next. Like, do I go back home and continue pretending nothing is wrong?"

Esther makes a disgusted face. "You shouldn't pretend anything at all, Chloe. Why don't you sit him down and just talk this shit out?"

Sam and Piper nod at this. Sam shrugs. "Not that I'm super at following my own advice, but it's always better to just have it out. Do your yelling rather than hide in your office and work until you forget to eat."

We all laugh a bit at the hypocrisy of Sam telling me this when she has a long history of locking herself in her coding cave to avoid her emotions. I feel my phone vibrate again and I'm not sure what makes me look at it this time, but I glance down to see the message is not from Teddy—it's from my tenants.

> SO sorry for the sudden notice. We closed early on the house. Yay! We're moving out this weekend. Obviously we'll keep paying the rent until you find someone. Wanted to let you know it's empty and see where to drop keys...

"Hm." I tap my lip with an index finger. The timing feels fortuitous to me. I'm hopping mad at my husband, sick of driving to the suburbs I hate, and wanting to feel in control of my life. The house will need to be repainted and cleaned before we can get tenants, at minimum.

I can spend some time there and sort out my thoughts,

figure out what I need. Maybe even call Lucy about playing some soccer. "I think I'm going to move back into my old house."

10

TEDDY

Now

"What do you mean you're going to go stay at the old house?" I feel like someone just kicked me in the solar plexus. Is my wife seriously telling me she's leaving me?

Chloe throws her hands in the air. "I can't live like this anymore, Teddy. We don't talk." I open my mouth to protest and she waves a hand around. "We calendar and we coordinate, but we don't talk. I just need some space."

"This is more than space." She is currently stomping around our bedroom tossing clothes into a giant suitcase. "Chloe, there has to be something in between not talking and you moving out."

"The house is going to be vacant, Teddy. We can't just have our property sitting around vacant."

"So we hire a damn property manager! This is something we can throw money at, Chloe. I need you."

She stops and stares at me, her hands on her hips.

"What do you need me for, Teddy? To look good on your arm at client dinners? To smile in the photo on your desk?"

"Chloe, that's not fair. Come on. You're my ... you're my everything."

She shakes her head. "Maybe I used to be. Now I'm just a bullet point on your resume or something." She zips up the bag and starts dragging it behind her. It thumps down the steps and I try to pick up the back end to help her. She snarls, but I don't let go.

I haven't lived apart from her since I was 20 years old. "I don't know how to be without you, Chloe."

She blows a tuft of brown hair up from her eyes. "Well, maybe you need to figure that out." She kicks the bag toward the front door and heads into her office. She looks around the room, grabs the box full of paperbacks, and starts to head for the door.

"I'll come with you to the house," I plead, placing a hand on the door so she can't open it.

"And then what? Leave this house unattended?"

"I don't care about the house!"

Her eyes flare. "That's news to me, considering you bought it despite me telling you I hate it." That stings. This house purchase has always been a sore spot. I know that impact matters more than intent and all that, but honestly when I started hearing about the schools up here, I just got so excited to begin our family with Chloe. To give the very best I could to our kids. I didn't want my kids growing up in a tiny school in an agricultural area where nobody had clothes that fit.

I assumed she'd love the house, and I set things up with the realtor. I didn't ask Chloe about moving, because I thought she always wanted this sort of life.

But of course, Chloe felt yanked from our home, unconsulted. She later yelled that there were Nobel laureates who graduated from the public schools of Pittsburgh. That just because something is the "best" on paper doesn't mean everything else is garbage.

I close my eyes and lean on the door. "Tell me what you need, Chloe."

"Space, Bear. I need some space and then I need you to fucking *talk* to me."

"I'm sorry about the shit with the soccer guys. I fucked up, Chloe. I admit that."

"This is much bigger than just that and you know it." She nudges me out of the way with her shoulder and heaves the suitcase down the front step toward her car. The bag takes off ahead of her, rolling with the momentum of the sloped walk. I shouldn't laugh, but it all feels so ridiculous, my amazing wife in such a hurry to get away from me that her possessions are running ahead of her.

Chloe can't lift the bag into the trunk of her car and I quietly walk behind her and heft it in. "Thank you." She stoops for her box of books, but I grab that, too, lifting with my back and knowing I'll regret it in the morning since I'm still sore from pickup soccer.

"Can I at least follow you in my car and help you get the bag in the house?" Chloe takes a deep breath through her nose and then nods.

AN HOUR later we stand in the empty rooms of the house we remodeled ourselves. I wish I shared Chloe's pride at the drywall we hung, at the chipped wooden stairs. "Chloe, babe, you can't camp here. There's no...things. You need things."

She scrunches up her face and looks around the empty kitchen. "I'll go to the resale store for some stuff."

"What about furniture? Where will you write?"

She seems pleased that I acknowledged her work in this way and I take note of that fact, that writing is the first thing on Chloe's mind, above a bed or pots and pans. "I'll sit at the counter, I guess. And maybe I'll follow you back to the house and grab a camping cot."

"You can't sleep on a cot."

"It's not forever, Teddy." A lump forms in my throat when she says that. I nod my head, fighting back tears. I have to cling to that assertion from her: that this is temporary. That this will only last as long as she can stand sleeping on a canvas cot.

I stand around awkwardly, waiting for her to invite me to stay or come with her to buy plates, but she just taps her foot and looks around. I reach for her hand and she stiffens.

"Can we try therapy? Can we work on this together?"

Chloe nods, an almost imperceptible tilt of her head, but I run with it. "I'll send you some options," I promise.

She doesn't ask me to stay, and so I don't.

On the drive back to the suburbs, back to the perfect school district for kids I can't sire, I allow myself a few tears. Unsurprisingly, I don't feel better after they fall. Something has to change.

11

CHLOE

THE FIRST DAY alone in the house, all I did was scrub walls with a magic eraser. My thoughts swirled all over the place as I scoured away grease stains in the kitchen and mildew from the bathrooms.

The second day, all I did was remember buying this house with Teddy. We were 22, newly married. Young and dumb, I think Esther would say. But I didn't feel dumb at the time. I felt like I was in on a Grand Plan, both of us with job offers and a special bank loan for first-time homeowners. Teddy absolutely refused to accept help from my parents for the down payment.

I wince, remembering how I felt like I might throw up telling my Dad we couldn't accept his offer. I think I only got half the sentence out before he shook his head and said he was sticking the money in some sort of trust in my name and that was that. I guess I should look into that account. It seemed easier to ignore it, not have to fight with Teddy or my Dad.

Today, I agreed to meet Teddy at a therapist's office in the city. He doesn't push back about trying to find someone closer to the house. I've stopped thinking of it as "our" house. Thinking of the gifted, secret money, I realize our problems began way before the infertility. I guess housing should probably top the list of things we discuss with a therapist. Or is this a finances thing? The therapist will know how to categorize it, I guess.

I'm actually able to walk to the office in Shadyside, just about a mile from our Highland Park house. The stroll feels nice on this crisp day, even if the sky is overcast. I always think better when I move my body. It's part of the reason sports have always been so important to me.

I know from Teddy's text that the therapist is named Pam but I have no additional information apart from her address. I frown, realizing we're meeting in someone's personal home where she evidently also conducts business. That seems awfully unsafe, for a woman to invite quarreling married couples into her private home.

I note the small ENTER sign above the door handle and step inside a living room. There's no sign of Teddy. I bite my lip and check the time on my phone, but I hear a voice say, "Chloe? Is that you? Come join us!"

I follow the sound around a corner to a more stereotypical therapist's office with a couch, two beanbag chairs, and a wooden perch type thing, upon which a woman with short gray hair is kneeling. "Would you care to join your husband on the couch?" She smiles at me and adjusts her weight.

Seeing me staring, she explains, "It's called a kneeling chair. It's good for my circulation." As if that settles the matter, she smiles, waiting for me to sit. It feels like a test, like if I sit next to Teddy we still have hope...but also if I sit next to my husband maybe we don't really need to be here? "Wherever you feel comfortable, Chloe. Even the floor!"

I sigh and sink into a beanbag, pulling my water bottle

from my bag and chugging a few swigs. Pam smiles. "Teddy arrived a few moments early and was telling me some things—"

"Typical," I snort. I clench my insides. I'm never impertinent. I don't interrupt people. But honestly, how dare he arrive early to our first session and tip the scales in his favor? Who even knows what he said.

Pam smiles again. "He was telling me some things and I asked to wait until you were here before we discussed what brought you two to my practice." She folds her hands on her lap. "Would either of you like to begin?"

I shut my water bottle noisily and slam it on the ground by my feet. I grip my thighs and say, "Teddy bulldozed our life plans, found out he's got a low sperm count, and has refused to discuss it."

His eyes widen and he adjusts his tie before retorting, "Chloe has a secret career writing dirty books and doesn't tell me when anything is wrong, except to say she was moving out."

We glare at one another as Pam nods. "Hm. Lots going on there for sure."

Suddenly, all the hurts just start bubbling out of me like a bath bomb dropped in water. "He told our college friends it's *me* who's infertile, he bought a house in the suburbs without asking me first. I feel like I'm an item on his checklist when I used to feel like we were partners." I take a deep breath as Teddy's mouth works up and down. "What happened to 'Team Presto,' huh? Team captains have meetings, last I checked. I barley even see you anymore."

"Team Presto?" Pam tilts her head, looking to Teddy for clarification.

He swallows thickly and runs his hands along his thighs. "When we were dating, I, um, got nervous about proposing.

I had a whole plan, a whole romantic proposal. And...I choked and just blurted 'want to form Team Presto and make it official?'" He looks at me and smiles, a thin-lipped little line. "You looked so happy when I asked that."

"I was. Then." I can't meet his eye so I stare at the artwork on Pam's wall. Lots of bridges through fog and hands extending toward the viewer. Deep metaphors all over this place.

"Hmm." Pam taps her finger on her notebook. "Chloe, do you remember when you first began to feel *un*happy? You and Teddy have been married for some time now."

Almost ten years. We got married right after undergrad. I didn't see the sense in waiting, and Teddy was keen for us to file our taxes jointly once we both had job offers. I thought it was endearing then, how he focused on the practical, economic benefits of one shared health insurance payment and hefty tax deductions.

"I loved our house in the city." My voice is quieter than I thought, so I try again a bit louder. "I still love it. That's where I'm staying now that our renters moved out."

"Renters I didn't even want—we needed to sell that place and get the cash."

My eyes flash at Teddy. "Cash for the house you didn't ask me before buying!"

"It's not like you could have been on the mortgage! You don't even have a job."

I cross my arms and look at Pam, waiting for her to step in and point out the horror of what Teddy just revealed. She does not.

I take a deep breath and clutch at my chest. "It's hurtful to hear you say that, both that I don't deserve a say in where we live unless I meet some criteria, and that you don't understand my work."

"What work? You were researching houses for people part-time. Now you're writing romance novels? How is that a viable career, Chloe? Where's the stability?"

"Oooh kayyy." Pam claps her hands together. "I'm just going to pause and reframe. Teddy, I heard Chloe say she felt hurt when you made a major marital property purchase without her input. I heard her say she feels undervalued."

"Yes!" I pick up my water and take a triumphant swig, but Pam taps her knee and turns to me.

"Chloe, I hear Teddy saying he feels shut out. That you aren't sharing your aspirations or your work with him."

"Did he say that, though?"

His face brightens and he nods. "Shut out. That's right. I don't know anything Chloe is thinking. About pregnancy stuff, about job stuff...all of it is a mystery."

"Mmm hmmm. Okay." Pam begins writing in her notebook. "Let's go back to your city house. Chloe, tell Teddy what you like about it."

Everything? How to even begin with such a question. I flip the water bottle lid around in my lap nervously. "I loved plastering the ceilings together. I held all the stuff and directed while Teddy reached up from the ladder to patch the cracks and it just felt so good to do something like that together, to make such a visible improvement." Pam nods. "We also pulled out about a million carpet staples before we re-oiled the hardwood floors. Remember? We crawled around listening to Green Day and pried up staples. And we had special tools to do it. I called it a bear claw, because Teddy is...my bear." My cheeks flush at the memory, especially when I remember Teddy yanking the bear claw from my hand and mauling me on the floor, making passionate love to me amidst the construction debris before we dabbed ourselves clean-ish and kept working into the night.

"It sounds like you both put a lot of work into making the home your own." Pam smiles. I nod. Teddy stares at the art.

I don't know when he lost that fierce determination, or redirected it toward something I couldn't see...but the new house feels very different. And I never wanted anything to do with it, even as I signed my name on all the closing papers. "The new house feels like a trap," I whisper. "A huge, open concept trap keeping me from the place I felt most comfortable."

12

TEDDY

I CAN'T DECIDE how to feel about the art on our marriage therapist's walls. There's a giant photograph of hands outstretched. I'm assuming they're meant to imply a helping hand, reaching toward someone who needs a lift to their feet.

Something about the hand reminds me of my father. His hand extended that way wouldn't have been to assist. He'd gesture like that to admonish, to spout anger at the way different groups were screwing him over...screwing him out of better pay or more benefits. You name it, someone else was at fault for it, not doing it right, or acting like a "sissy."

As if acting like a woman is some weakness. I think about my mother, never complaining through hard work, her hands gnarled from harsh chemicals and long hours. Is she a sissy?

I listen to my wife reminisce about our early days in the house we bought and I remember how anxious I felt about those home repairs, knowing that there was no money then to hire someone. Chloe had been so impressed I had all those skills—spackle and caulk and a few turns of a screwdriver.

"You called me a Handy Bear," I mutter, still staring at the hands.

"You were handy, Teddy. You knew how to get our house ready for us to live there comfortably."

I meet Chloe's gaze where she sits in the damn bean bag, across the room from me. "I preferred paying someone else to do those things in our current home." I cross my arms across my chest and look away from the hands art. I notice brush strokes in the ceiling paint, where someone has obviously been in recently to do a repair. Probably water damage. I wish it didn't make me so uncomfortable to know that, and I don't understand why it does.

Pam leans forward a bit at my words. "Can you tell us more about that preference, Teddy?"

I consider her question. "It seems...better, to be able to outsource those things. To walk into a house and just have to put away your clothes and hang your art." I wish I hadn't mentioned the art because now I'm looking at the hands again.

"Hm, so you like being taken care of?"

I shift my gaze to the therapist. "I don't think that's what I meant." I think about it a little more. "I like being able to afford to pay someone to take care of things."

Pam makes notes in her book and then slams it shut and stands, stretching. "You two have worked really hard today. I know it hasn't been a long session, but you've shared some very big feelings and I know you must be exhausted. I'd like to give you a homework assignment before next week."

Chloe's face brightens at this. She likes assignments. Give her a specific list of things to achieve and off she goes, cheerfully meeting her goals. Just not when I make the list. Maybe it's all about the delivery. I don't know anymore.

"For homework," Pam continues, "I want you to sit down together and ask each other about work—recent highlights, what a typical day looks like, where you'd like to be in a year, that sort of talk."

"Work?" I feel my face contort in surprise. "I thought we were going to focus on the stuff we fight about."

"We don't fight," Chloe mumbles. "We ignore…"

Pam nods again. "It sounds like work is a big part of each of your identity and you've gotten out of the habit of discussing the particulars with one another. Let's start with some conversations about work and build up to these other areas of conflict." She smiles. "Same time next week?"

OUTSIDE, Chloe takes a swig from her water bottle shielding her eyes from the glare. Her eyes have always been very sensitive to light, even on gray days like today. I look around for her car and don't see it. I clear my throat. "Are you parked far away?"

"I walked." Her voice is flat, lacking any of her usual politeness.

I scratch my neck and resist the urge to look at my watch. "Can I walk you home?"

This seems to surprise her but she shrugs and heads north toward our old house…her current house. I don't even know what to call it. I take a deep breath. "So, I've been having a lot of meetings with my team recently. We renewed a few contracts…Yvonne got some leads on a new client."

"That's great." Chloe's voice is flat, like she doesn't give a shit, which pisses me off.

"So you're just going to half-ass our homework? You, Chloe 'perfect' Preston?"

"Ugh. Fine." She stops walking and faces me. "I'm glad you like your job." Her tone is clipped but borders on pleasant.

"Well. Thanks. I do like it, Chloe. It's really stable. This company's going places."

"What does that mean to you, Teddy? Going places? Literally travel? More hours?"

"It should be less travel now." I kick at some acorn tops on the sidewalk, wondering if a squirrel is going to hurl nuts at me from a utility pole or something. "So I should be home more."

I want her to tell me that would be nice, that she wants to spend more time with me. She used to tell me she missed me, that it was hard when I worked such long hours...but I had to secure this promotion. I had to show that I could put in the time, that I was dedicated to our clients. Somewhere in there, she stopped missing me, I guess.

"Will you, uh, tell me about becoming Chloe Petals?" An arched brow from my wife has my heart racing. She's so fucking beautiful. Even more beautiful than when I first met her, more mature and confident.

"You heard the gist of it at Fuel and Fuddle." She kicks an acorn toward me, and I trap it like a soccer ball, passing it back to her. She smiles and passes it back again and I feel lighter inside, a glimmer of hope.

"I want to hear about your work, Chlo. I'll listen this time." I know she's mentioned it before. She probably emphasized it was important to her. I probably wasn't able to focus because I was gung ho about my own work.

I reach for her hand as we cross Penn Avenue. It feels

silly, but she used to always reach for me at busy intersections. I grew up in a rural place without stoplights. Chloe jokes that I'll get run over by a scooter if she doesn't help me cross big roads. She hooks a pinky around my thumb, the rest of her fingers clutching her water bottle.

Once we're on the curb, she says, "There were so many stories with the house histories. Scorned lovers and inheritance disputes. Bathtub accidents." She takes a sip of water and offers me the bottle. I shake my head. "I came across a really old deed when I was doing a history for that house in Verona. You know the one that's an AirBNB?" I shake my head again.

She sighs. "Well, anyway, I started really wondering what the area was like in the 18th century, what the people's lives would have been like...I just wanted to make a story for them. It sort of snowballed and then I knew I had a book." Chloe squints as she looks both ways to cross, despite the four-way stop. I'll never have those sorts of instincts...I'd just trust that the cars would drive slowly enough to see us coming. Chloe thinks I act like I have blinders on, but a lot of the time I just assume people will behave differently. She knows city drivers hate stopping. I grew up waving to pedestrians because I knew them all. "Samantha and Nicole were the ones who encouraged me to talk to Emma Stag about independent publishing."

"Independent? What's that mean?"

She holds out her hands, much like the gesture in the picture from Pam's office. "It means I do everything. Cover design, hire an editor, market the book...produce the audio, solicit reviews. Everything."

"How do you know how to do all that?" I stop walking to stare at her. I never took a minute to think about the process of getting a book from a Word file into a tattered paperback that lives in a friend's duffel bag.

"I learned, Teddy. I learned an awful lot."

13

CHLOE

11 Years Ago

I BLINK, certain I misheard my boyfriend. "You want to move in together?"

He nods. "It makes sense. We're both extremely busy and it takes a lot of time packing a bag each time I sleep at your place. Plus I don't think your roommates appreciate having me in the apartment so much."

I shrug. "So we can stay at your place more often. Don't you like sleeping in your own bed on game nights?"

Teddy shakes his head. "Only because it sucks cramming into a twin with two people. I've thought it all out, Chloe. We can get a one-bedroom apartment, pay less than we each are paying in rent now, and spread ourselves out in a king-sized bed. Think of the space!"

"We're twenty years old. I don't even know what I want to do after college. You want us to move in together?" I run my fingers along the seams of my soccer shorts over and over. This all feels so sudden, but I can tell Teddy is getting agitated as I resist his idea.

"I love you, Chloe." He smiles and rests a hand on my thigh. We are perched on my twin bed in my tiny room, his knee bumping against my dresser, which is scattered with his spare toiletries.

"I love you, too, Bear." And it's true. I love his quiet determination. I love how he takes things seriously, helps us set good schedules for studying and homework. I haven't missed a single assignment since we started dating and he taught me about color-coding my calendar for each class.

Teddy is so driven. He adjusts his posture and yelps when his knee really hits the corner of the dresser. I wince. "Space would be nice," I admit. "But where is there a spacious one-bedroom in our price range?"

His face brightens. "I already found a place! It's outside a reasonable walk-radius to campus, but there are regular buses and it's in a quiet neighborhood so we can sleep on game-nights without barflies waking us up."

My eyes widen. "When did you have time to do all this re-con?"

He shrugs and stands up. "Come on," he says. "I'll show you the building."

We hop on an eastbound bus away from campus, riding along Fifth Ave well past all the college-friendly apartment buildings, past Mellon park, and into a real neighborhood. "There are actual people here," I whisper, seeing folks with baby strollers and dogs. Teddy grins and nods.

The bus crosses Penn Ave and he pulls the cord for us to get off. He tugs my hand along Thomas Blvd, a wide street with flowered medians and huge mansions that have been sub-divided into apartments. "This is really nice, Bear. This is affordable?" In the Oakland neighborhood closer to campus, anything without cigarette butts on the stairwell is too expensive.

He spins on the sidewalk a few houses in from the corner. An old house towers above us, its stone facade in need of a scrub but in otherwise amazing shape. "It doesn't even smell like beer," I whisper, waving at a little girl skipping down the sidewalk toward her parents. "They have a swing set in the yard."

"I knew you'd love it." Teddy drapes an arm around my shoulder and pulls me tight against him. This is a neighborhood for real adults. The people parking their cars emerge in suits and ties, carrying briefcases, returning from work in real offices.

I bite my lip. Our dingy apartment buildings seem like a rite of passage for a college student. But Teddy obviously spent hours researching this place, thinking of all different aspects. How come he didn't tell me he was pondering any of this? "Isn't a little soon for us to level up to this sort of place?"

He recoils. "Why? Why not build a life that works for us? Think of it, Chloe. Grocery shopping together, cooking meals together...we can make ten sandwiches on Sunday evenings and have our lunches packed for the week. And look—this place has a covered porch." He points up to the second floor of the house, to a little wooden deck. "We can grow things, babe." He elbows me in the ribs. "We can grow plants with roots, like our relationship."

I roll my eyes. "Very cheesy, sir."

He squeezes my hand. "But we *could* toss our shin guards and smelly cleats out there overnight. Please tell me you'll think about it." I nod my head. Of course I'll consider it. I just...am not as certain as he is that I'm ready to put my wild days behind me for this adult life he's proposing. Not that

I'm so wild. We're both dedicated athletes and students. We don't party too hard. Maybe that's why I want to cling to life close to campus, just to bask in the atmosphere a bit longer.

Teddy gives my hand a firm squeeze. "Just maybe think about it by Friday because we'd have to sign a lease and start gathering a downpayment." He grins sheepishly and I swat him in the chest.

As we walk back to the bus stop I think about the sense of his plan. What's the alternative? Another year with non-romantic roommates? It's not like I enjoy sleeping apart from Teddy. Even if we're not having sex, it's nice to fall asleep in his arms, to feel the solid presence of him in my bed. And I hate spending the night at his place. He's tidy, but Noah and Judah are always spilling food and leaving sticky trails behind them. Plus the carpet smells weird at his apartment. I don't want to spend another year smelling weird carpet.

"I'll do it," I say, leaning my head on Teddy's shoulder.

He squeaks in excitement and wraps both arms around me, kissing the top of my head. "I'll take care of everything," he says, giving me a squeeze. "You don't have to worry about a thing."

14

CHLOE

Now

I STARE at my email in disbelief. A real literary agent wants me to give her a call about a publishing deal for my books. I've never even been to New York City, but this woman is offering to fly me there, put me up in a hotel, and sit down with fancy publishing executives.

I think about Emma Stag, my friend from Foof who publishes independently after having a "regular" book deal like this agent is offering. From what Emma was saying, the publisher can reach a huge audience, but they're also in charge of the book prices. I made my big break when book two came out and I put book one on sale.

I continue looking at the email, tapping my nails on the table until my alarm goes off, reminding me I'm supposed to meet my husband for therapy homework. My marriage has become so strange. We live in separate houses, ignore each other for most of the week, and then snarl out all our grievances at therapy.

This week, Pam sent us off to buy a plant and care for it together.

"I just don't know if this will help." Teddy and I stand staring at a row of house plants at the nursery near our city house. "We're not even staying in the same space. How are we supposed to co-parent a plant?"

Teddy fingers the yellowing leaves of a pothos. "This one says it's pretty impossible to kill."

I roll my eyes. "Oh that's a great bar to set." He grins. We've always enjoyed high expectations. How could we not, when we met as division one college athletes? When we told the clerk we were looking for a house plant to keep alive, he steered us toward a section of what he called 'low intervention" plants.

"What if I came over every-other day and watered it? I could bring dinner."

That sounds like more dinners eaten together than we usually have when we're living in our suburb house. I feel my irritation rise when I think about how much damn time he's spending in the car every day. Time we could be caring for plants, apparently.

I close my eyes and grip the edge of the shelf full of spider plants. "I don't want an easy plant. I want a challenge, something we actually work on together. With a strategy."

He arches a brow and leans against the shelf. "You mean you want to win, and the game is horticulture?"

I hold up my hands and tap my foot. "I guess so? I didn't set the homework."

He hooks a thumb over his shoulder toward the orchids. "You saying you want to propagate vanilla beans together, Chloe?" I'm not sure why it's annoying to me that he's enjoying this. Why can't I just relax and have fun with him?

I shake my head and march off to a different aisle,

looking at a cactus display. I'm prickly and tender. In our session today we talked a lot about how Teddy lost my trust when he just sprang the new house on me, how I've felt like an afterthought ever since.

Sure, I can see what he's saying about wanting the best and the most comfortable life because he never had that. But the way he went about it still stings. "Not a cactus, babe. Please." I hadn't realized he came up behind me, but there he is, looking over my shoulder at a succulent called a rat tail.

I bite my lip and nod, wandering to the next section of the store. I pause in front of a big display of "grow at home" kits. Teddy pokes at an herb garden. "Hey, if I'm coming over for dinner, what about herbs? We could add fresh basil and parsley to things we cook."

"That's a nice idea." I lean close and study the boxes, but I find it off-putting the way they all seem to emphasize that even a child could grow these things. "I still like the idea of growing something tricky. Something we have to troubleshoot."

Teddy walks around to the side of the display and holds up a box to grow mushrooms. "What about fungi?"

WE WALK OUT of the store holding a package of shiitake starter, which the clerk assured me was next-level mushroom growing. Anyone can grow a flush of pink oysters or lion's mane, apparently. But the shiitakes take effort. This pleases me.

I don't want to do the sensible thing for once, or purchase the plant that seems to make sense. I want this—a smelly log of finicky mushrooms that will require real effort.

"I'm glad you still want to take on a challenge with me,"

he says, swinging the bag as we walk toward the house. It should feel like a victory, a moment of connection, but all I can think about is the email from the agent. Some stranger in New York has read my work and studied my sales ranks and my own husband doesn't even know what my books are about. How can I trust him to tend to a mushroom when he doesn't tend to me? I frown. "What?" He stops walking. "What did I say?"

"You should read one of my books, Teddy. Or at least listen to the audio."

"You want me to listen to a sexy dude read me your sexy books?"

I purse my lips. It feels like the least he can do, but I also feel like he should want to do it. Should have wanted to read them ages ago. We walk a few blocks in silence.

"You're absolutely right," he says, finally. "This is important and I'll read them. I promise."

I take a deep breath and nod, climbing the porch steps to unlock the front door.

The inside is slightly less cavernous now. I found a pair of armchairs and a coffee table at the thrift store and a box of dinged up pots and pans and dishes.

I've long since finished repainting the walls and I told Isla and Julian not to worry about the rent. It seemed unfair to charge them when I'm living here.

Teddy puts the mushroom kit on the counter and I reach for it, intending to rip it open and get started. He sets a hand on my wrist. "Wait. Babe, it says to watch the instruction video online before you open the box."

"There's not instructions inside the box? What if I didn't have access to the internet?"

"Then you wouldn't have bought a shiitake kit, I imagine." He shrugs out of his coat and drapes it over the stool at the counter before propping his phone up on the mushroom box. We watch the guy in the video talk about stringy white mushroom "seeds," which Teddy insists we call by their proper name: mycelium.

After the video, I reach for the box again, ready to jump in, but Teddy says we should watch the video one more time. I sigh. It's always been like this, him studying and approaching everything methodically. Me erratically moving on instinct. Both strategies served us well...until they didn't anymore, I guess.

I used to think these differences helped us function. Now I'm just bored watching *again* as the video guide emphasizes the importance of humidity for growing this type of mushroom.

Together, we ease the block of sawdust from the box. It looks moldy to me, streaked with white inside the plastic wrapper. I wrinkle my nose at the smell. Teddy shakes his head. "I don't think this looks like the picture on the box. It says to wait until the log is mostly brown."

I frown at it. "You're right. Ugh. How long will it take?" With another shrug, Teddy reaches for his phone. "What are you looking up now?" I stretch up to try and see what he's doing.

"I'm ordering dinner, Chloe. You want meatballs or tacos?"

15

TEDDY

CHLOE and I agreed I'd come over every-other day to talk about fungus. Which leaves me feeling lost on the days between. It's not good for me to be alone. I'm not sleeping, just ruminating.

Down time is still pretty new to me. There's no such thing on a farm, and college was a blur of managing training, competition, and academics. Then Chloe and I had house projects to eat up our time after work.

I rub a hand across my neck, thinking of the house. I look around at this house, the new construction with walls that haven't yet had time to crack. All the appliances are efficient, all the walls are insulated, and I don't have to do a god-damned thing to maintain it. Is it possible I miss tinkering with old plumbing?

More likely I just miss Chloe.

I pace around the house for a bit, and decide to make my monthly phone call to check in with my parents. My mom answers as she usually does. "Yep? Everything good?"

"Hey, Mom. Things are fine. You busy?" It sounds like she's washing dishes.

"Well, we moved the birds today. Hired help was late of course."

I groan, both because I remember how laborious it is to move the chickens from the pullet barn to the barn where they'll finish growing...and because I know my mother's comment is a dig about me not being there. They wouldn't have to hire help if I stuck around the family business. I reach for something I could say, something we could have a conversation about.

I try to imagine Chloe living with me on a farm, and I realize I wouldn't have even met Chloe if I'd stayed there.

"Here's your father," Mom says, and a muffled sound indicates she's passing him the phone.

"Hey, Dad. Birds all get moved?"

"Barely, yep. You take over that office of yours yet?"

I frown. Did I forget to tell them I got the promotion or is he making small talk? No wonder my wife and I are estranged. I have no idea how to talk to people I care about. "I'm doing okay at work, Dad. We got a new contact this week."

"New contracts are good if you can deliver." I hear him suck air through his teeth.

I should tell him I always deliver, that he taught me to always finish the job. But I don't know how to say any of that. "You and Mom going to finally come see the new house this winter?" I know before I ask that he's going to say 'maybe' and that they won't make the trip. They haven't been to the city since we got married. Chloe and I usually make a visit out to the farm once or twice a year...during cycles when there's nothing major happening on the farm.

"We'll see," Dad says. And then, "Well, I'm going to let you go."

"Okay, Dad. Good talking to you."

"You, too, son." And then he's gone, and I feel more alone than I did before I called.

I CONSIDER GOING FOR A RUN, actually lace up my sneakers and step outside, and then I see what Chloe has been saying. There aren't sidewalks in our subdivision, and it's not like I can run on the street. Folks just aren't looking out for random joggers as they drive home from work.

I should probably call her and cede that point, build some trust. Then I worry that I'll be bothering her while she's thinking and I talk myself out of even that. Should I email Chloe to ask about a set time each day to talk on the phone?

Jesus. I've lived with Chloe for a decade-plus. Now we're reduced to an email about a standing one on one? She'd hate that. What if, even worse, our conversations turn into the sort of non-conversations I have with my parents?

With a sigh, I climb into my car and start driving. I head into the city, back toward my office, but decide to swing through the Oakland neighborhood, by the soccer stadium at the university. I can't see much from the street, but the stadium lights indicate the teams are probably in there practicing.

I miss the routine of that, the comfort of knowing no matter what was going on there would always be 30 guys running around, sweating, giving each other shit. I swing back down the hill and park near Fuel n Fuddle. I walk inside before I can think better of it, a thirty-something guy all alone in a college bar.

I sink into a stool and order whatever beer is on special today. I make it a few sips in silence before I feel self-conscious and pull out my phone like everyone else. Biting my lip, I wonder if it's late enough that I wouldn't risk disturbing Chloe's work by messaging her. I decide to text her about the shiitake.

> Any nubbins yet?

CHLOE PRESTON:
> You know it's called fruiting!

> Don't leave me hanging over here, Chlo.

It's a strange feeling, flirting with my own wife. I like it. I take another sip of the beer, deciding it's terrible. You get what you pay for, as always.

CHLOE PRESTON:
> No signs of life. I feel like there should be something by now, right?

> We can troubleshoot at dinner tomorrow.

I bite my cheek. This is me being daring, assuming she'll have dinner with me, if only for the sake of the mushroom log.

CHLOE PRESTON:
> I have Foof tomorrow.

My heart sinks. Of course I don't want her to miss her night with her friends. I know how much they mean to her. Honestly, I wish I had a group like that. People who have my back like my teammates used to. I stare at the shitty beer and shake my head.

> I'll come early for breakfast, then. Before work.

She writes back almost immediately.

CHLOE PRESTON:

Gasp! You'll skip out on fancy chef food??

I smile. She's definitely flirting back.

Our fungi depend on it, babe.

I toss a few bills on the bar and head for home.

16

CHLOE

I'M surprised by how much I think about this mushroom log. It has definitely become a focal point for me. I could lie and say it's because I don't have a television here, but the truth is I really want to succeed at growing a shiitake mushroom. I'd be happy with one.

That's a lie. I want a full flush of them, as the package calls it. I'm glad Teddy and I took our homework assignment in our own direction, and I'll admit I've been enjoying having a shared goal with him again. I want the mushroom project to work out because that would mean this marriage project can work out. I really don't think I envisioned a scenario otherwise. I didn't move here to this house because I want to divorce him. I don't even know what life looks like without Teddy.

All I know is right now, this fungus project is the only thing keeping us going.

We still haven't talked about the Big I, but at least we've talked about more than just our schedules.

I smile, remembering our text exchange from last night. I was surprised he slipped in a spontaneous breakfast invite.

Last-minute plans never sit well with Teddy. Unless the change comes from his office, I think miserably.

I remind myself that he's gotten used to getting his way about everything from where we live to, apparently, when we discuss mushrooms. And then I remind myself that he was pretty quick to suggest a compromise when I said no to dinner tonight. It feels good to set a boundary and claim this time for my meeting.

Ordinarily, I'd be brimming with excitement to share work news with the gals. I just completed a second draft of my third book and sent it off to my advance readers. I even picked a publication date and set up the pre-orders to lure in people who finished book two.

Today, I get to spend hours fiddling with the text on the ads I want to run for my series. I love tweaking images and finding just the right words to tempt readers into my steamy historical romance.

Even lesbians love it, I try, thinking of Jenny and her wife rereading my battered paperback. *Prime your powder. This pistol is hot!*

"Okay this is going to take some work." My words echo a bit off the empty walls. I'm not producing my best creative work here. I do miss my cheerful office with the cozy carpet. Maybe I should go back and grab my ball chair at least.

Then I remember the email from the agent. Could I let a publishing company handle all these ads instead? Let them pay me a huge advance to just write the books while publishing staffers bring them to bookshelves?

For a solid minute, I imagine myself living a totally different life as a fancy author in a bigger city, with an agent and a publisher and "people" doing my bidding.

And then I remember that I do have people. I have an editor I chose, a narrator I found after scouring the web and listening to samples. I have friends here. And Teddy, of course. There's always Teddy.

This isn't just a life I fell into. I have choices here.

I sigh, because even though it's difficult, I really enjoy my author business. I do all the work...and I get all the pride, creative control and royalties. I look at the agent's email again—she has sent me a few nudges.

Hi Danielle, I type. *Thank you so much for reaching out. At this time, I'm not looking for a publishing contract. Can I keep you in mind if that changes in the future?*

I click send before I second-guess myself, and dive back into my ads. These books aren't going to sell themselves. I've overcome greater challenges than cavernous rooms impeding my creativity.

MY ALARM SOUNDS for me to get ready for Foof, and I stretch, realizing happily that several hours have passed without my noticing. That certainly never happened when I had the office job. I used to avoid checking the time because so little of it would have passed. Now, much like when I used to get immersed in training for soccer, the hours just seem to fly by. "I'm in the zone, baby." I smile, recalling my former coach's voice when she'd have to shout my name to offer instruction. I just got so lost in playing.

I hum as I head to the bathroom to shower and change out of my yoga pants. I'm sure I *could* roll into Bridges and Bitters dressed like a work-from-home author, but I like looking cute once in a while.

As I dig around for my favorite dark jeans, I realize I don't really ever get dressed up for Teddy. I should probably bring that up with Pam. Why do I put effort into myself when I'm going out with friends, on my own, but not when

I'm looking to woo my husband? Did I stop caring about my appearance before or after he grew an iceberg where his libido once was?

I yank on the jeans with a dark green top and pull my hair into a loose braid. It's been a while since I wore any makeup at all, but I do find a tube of mascara and tinted lip gloss in the bottom of the bag I threw together when I left the suburbs. Red flats and a cardigan feel easy but I love the difference in my appearance from just these small changes. I shove my phone in my pocket and head out, feeling confident and excited to be among my friends.

As I drive to the bar, I think about how Foof feels a lot like a soccer team used to feel. A bunch of goal-oriented women who meet regularly and work hard, support each other. I can lean on these friends and know they'll push me to be better.

When I walk into Esther's space, I smile at the change of mood. She's in full autumn mode now, with deep red and orange decor and a chalk menu reflecting a new array of cocktails, plus some locally brewed beers for a change of pace.

I make my way up to the bar and lean on my elbows, studying the new options.

"What'll it be, Preston?" Esther winks at me as she shakes up a silver container for another patron.

"Since when do you have fancy beers?" I squint to look at the names. She usually just has some bottles of the big-name brands.

"My sister knows a gal," Esther says, pouring the drink and sliding it down the bar. "You wanna try one?"

I hesitate, because I do, but I also want to taste whatever Esther invented for us tonight and I can never remember what the rules are about mixing liquor and beer. Sensing my dilemma, Esther offers, "I just switched over to the new menu so I wasn't going to force any of you to taste anything new today."

I laugh at this. "Oh, yeah, we hate being your test kitchen," I deadpan. "Okay, I'll try the fancy IPA."

I TAKE my suds and make my way to the back room, where Nicole Brady and Sam Vine are literally wrestling over what appears to be a giant scepter. I lean in to Piper, who seems poised to intervene. "What are they doing?"

"Sam wanted to introduce a talking stick into the mix." Piper doesn't take her eyes off the pair as they tug on the silver baton. "Nicole feels this is unnecessary."

A few tense seconds pass before Juniper Jones, who was recently re-elected to her judge role, pulls a gavel from her purse and bangs it against the wall. "Order in the pub!"

This breaks the tension and Nicole sighs, releasing the heavy scepter. I'm impressed when Samantha doesn't fall. She extends herself to full height and smiles. "As I was saying! I thought we could try something new. I brought a power staff." She presents it like a *Price is Right* model. "I figure when someone from Foof feels particularly glorious, she could hold the staff over her head. Like She-Ra!"

We all nod in a chorus of understanding. I like this idea. I take a seat around the giant table as Piper reaches for the stick and excitedly shares that she started scoping out locations for her own business. "I have to have an exit plan from the gym," she says, banging the stick on her lap. "I'll wither up if I keep working there."

Nicole nods knowingly. "Let me know if a spreadsheet would help. I'm assuming you have your financials in order?"

Piper tosses one arm around Logan's shoulders and pulls her in close. "I definitely do. You all are seriously the best at encouraging me."

IN THE END, I don't share anything with the group. I listen as Sam and her new colleague Lyra talk about balancing work and personal life. I smile as Logan and Orla vent about childcare challenges. Even with on-site daycare at Vinea, Logan still runs into issues if she and her husband, Cal, both have somewhere to be in the evening.

My Foof friends are reproducing at a rapid pace these days, and the shift makes me wistful. I wasn't aware of these realities they're bringing up, because Teddy and I don't have kids. Might not be able to. I do notice a change in how I feel about the conversation, though. Instead of bitter disappointment or anger with my husband, I find myself wishing I could tell him about what Logan said. I wonder what his response would be or what sort of ideas he'd have about childcare.

I take that as a positive sign, and later, in my cot, I fall asleep excited to see him in the morning.

I'M LESS excited when he knocks on the door at six, though.

I pad down the hall, hair on top of my head, and squint through the window beside the door. "How early did you leave the house?" I shuffle back toward my cot as he bustles in the door. Rather than risk scuffing the wood upstairs I just set up my bed in the living room along with the arm chairs, so that's where Teddy situates himself with white paper bakery bags.

"There's no traffic this time of day. It was kind of amazing. You want a scone?"

I nod and hold a hand up, delighting in the scratchy feel of the turbinado sugar. As soon as it connects with my tongue, I feel a jolt of energy. It's enough to help me sit up and rub the sleep from my eyes. Teddy brushes crumbs from his dark tie, his knees spread wide in his navy slacks. I like how the low overhead light reflects on his shiny brown dress shoes. "You look nice, Bear."

He grins, the little crooked expression I've loved from the start. Taking another bite of his pastry, he points toward the kitchen. "Should we talk about the shiitake?"

I groan and struggle to stand, and am surprised when he extends a hand to help me up. I revel in his strong grip, feeling him tug me to my feet with ease. Huh.

We make our way to the kitchen and I set to work starting the coffee while he peers in closely and stares at the brown lump of substrate on the counter. "I think we might need to try a humidity tent."

"Elaborate."

He tells me how he watched more mushroom videos last night and thinks the problem might be the house's forced air heat. "The air in here is so dry! It's not the best time of year to start a mushroom flush, but I think we can make a tent."

He tells me how we can rig up a plastic grocery bag with some holes in it to trap in the moisture when we spray the log. "If we set it on the counter above the dishwasher, it'll be warmer, too."

I nod as he looks around for scissors and a shopping bag. "Oh, wait!" I remember the bag of grapes in the fridge and I dump the remaining fruit into a cereal bowl, flourishing the bag with its many ventilation holes. "How about this?"

"Amazing!" Teddy's delight is contagious and we finagle the grape bag over the project, lifting the bottom edge for the morning misting. He drapes an arm around my shoulders and I lean in to his warmth. "I kind of want to set up a camera to check in on it. Like a time lapse video or something."

"That's a little extreme, babe."

He nudges me with his shoulder. "Don't act like you're not excited. I can feel you vibrating."

"That's just the sugar," I lie. He's right. I am oddly thrilled by this development, working with him to come up with a new idea to approach this problem. Teddy bumps me with his shoulder again and I stick a thumb in one of his belt loops.

He stares at me, and for a minute I think he might kiss me. I think I might like that. But he doesn't do it. We look at each other for a long time, eyes dancing in the low light of the kitchen. The coffeemaker beeps to signal it's ready and it breaks the spell. Teddy steps to the side and pours himself a mug. "You promise you'll text me if anything happens?"

I nod. "Absolutely." He chugs the rest of his coffee and puts it in the sink, heading out the front door for work.

17

CHLOE

"YOU GOT ME A DOG?" I stare at the furry, vibrating ball circling my feet.

Teddy flushes. He leans against the door frame and scratches the back of his neck. "Do you like it? Him, I mean?" The dog looks up at me and pees on the hardwood floor. I whip my gaze to my husband, who winces. "He's a rescue," Teddy says, as if that explains the dog's presence and the urine likely staining my freshly-oiled pine boards.

Wordlessly, I turn on my heel and head for the kitchen in search of rags and a bottle of cleaner. When I return to the hall, Teddy is seated on the floor, resting his back against the wall and holding his fingers out toward the dog, who snarls at him. *Smart dog,* I think, unkindly.

As I stoop to clean up the pee, Teddy sighs. "I don't know why I keep doing the same thing wrong. I thought the dog would be a gesture." I can hear his air quotes around the word our marriage therapist uses for everything. *Everything is a gesture, symbolic.*

I drop the damp towel on the floor with a smack. "All I

see is a lot of work, Teddy. Am I supposed to stop writing every few hours to clean up pee? You know how hard I worked to get this place cleaned up."

Teddy stares at the dog as it sniffs its own pee. "I didn't want you to be alone in the house."

"So you got me a purse-dog?" I know I sound like a raging bitch. It's not my intention to fight with him. In fact, I moved into our little city house to get away from the fighting.

Maybe that's not true. I had to get away from the lack of fighting. From the silence and avoidance, and constantly feeling like a viewer in the suspense movie that is my own life. The dog hops into Teddy's lap and starts licking Teddy's face. I feel a twinge of happiness at the image, but it passes quickly. "Does he even have a name?"

Teddy strokes the dog's head and smiles at him. "I thought we could choose one together. I mean, he had one at the shelter, but I don't think he should keep that one."

I scrunch up my face as the dog wags its entire body under Teddy's ministrations. It must be some sort of Pekingese, all floof and tiny parts. "What were they calling him at the shelter?"

Teddy glances up at me. He clenches his jaw and swallows. He pets the dog a few more times before saying, quietly, "Baby. They called him Baby."

"Oh." I sink to the floor next to my estranged husband and the dog starts running back and forth between us, tongue flapping as he pants excitedly. "Yeah, we should change that." A glimmer of hope flashes across Teddy's face when I say the word 'we.' I purse my lips and stare at the dog. "Teddy, I don't know the first thing about caring for a dog. This really isn't a good time for me to take on a pet, especially with all the fresh paint and tung oil all over the house. Why wouldn't you talk to me about something like this before just...getting a dog?"

"Pam told me to buy you things," he snaps. "I took off work to do this, Chloe. I invested time into doing something kind for you. And I fucking know it was the wrong thing. The same impulsive thing I always do, but here we are."

I shake my head. "You might think this was kind and considerate, but you just dumped a literal shit ton of work on me, Teddy." The dog craps on the floor next to Teddy's leg and I gesture at the poop. "I don't think Pam told you to *buy* me things. I believe she asked you to think about what I might need and how you could offer it to me. And, I don't know, maybe *include me in the conversation about it!*"

He shakes his head and pinches his nose. "I'm lousy at this stuff." He gestures at the poop as the dog starts chewing Teddy's shoe. "So what do we do?"

"You take him back to your house and—"

"Our house," he interrupts. "It's *our* house. And so is this one."

My eyes feel like they're going to bulge out of my face. "Fine," I huff. "You take the dog to our McMansion and potty train him. I will stay here and continue spackling holes, and repainting walls. Dog free. Like we planned."

He leans forward, grabbing the bottle of cleaner and the rag. He looks at the turd on the floor and climbs to his feet. I watch as Teddy walks into the powder room, rips off some toilet paper, and picks up the mess, flushing it before squatting down to wipe the floor clean. "We didn't plan this, Chloe." His voice is muffled as he works.

Teddy's right about that. Nothing in the past few years has been *our* plan, collectively. But now doesn't feel like the time for me to remind him that he was the one who drained our savings to buy a house an hour drive up the highway from my friends, from my entire life in Pittsburgh. After our session last week and the mushroom dinner the other night, I thought we had made a breakthrough.

This dog purchase is just another major decision Teddy made without me.

As Teddy washes his hands in the powder room sink, I watch his fingers move. I've always loved his hands, his long digits with rough tips hewn from years landscaping and working in fields every summer up until his first *real job*, as he calls it.

"Is it okay to flush dog poop down the toilet?" I stare at the bathroom, with its 100-year-old pipes. I might actually combust if we have to replace anything else in this house right now.

Teddy scratches at his chin and stares at the dog. "I don't actually know."

I pull out my phone to look up the answer, and Teddy sits back down beside me, peering over my shoulder as we wait for the search engine to load. I used to cherish these moments of closeness with him, lean into him and soak up the smell of my handsome Teddy Bear. Now I just feel anxious, constantly holding my breath waiting for something else to explode.

I type in the question and we both sigh as the Internet tells us it should be okay to flush dog poop as long as it's not in a plastic bag. I shove my phone back in my jeans pocket. "That was a close call." Teddy winces as he says it, as if he's just now seeing a pattern in which he does things without thinking first and even if he means well, sets our lives on a rough path.

"Well." I stand up and brush my hair back from my face.

"Nice of you two to stop by, I guess. I really should get back to work." My voice drifts off as I stare at the dog, now chewing on the lip of the bottom step, his little teeth scratching into the tung oil finish. Teddy stoops to pick up the ball of fur and nods. Without another word, he walks out the front door.

18

TEDDY

THIS HALLWAY SMELLS OF DESPERATION. The fertility research clinic lives deep inside the women's hospital where most Pittsburghers go to have their babies. You know, just to make it a little bit more painful to enter the damn building. I walked past a woman obviously in labor on the way in here and because nothing is labeled, I had to circle the first floor twice.

I'll be damned if I stop and ask for directions to the fertility clinic. Why not just wear a sign around my neck. *Here goes Teddy Preston: No Viable Sperm.*

I wanted to wear a ball cap pulled down low, but since I'm here on my lunch break, decked out in a suit, I decided the hat would draw even more attention. I should have considered a fedora...that would have looked slick with my suit.

I'm not sure what made me email the clinic about finally scheduling a follow-up appointment. Something about that damn mushroom log, watching Chloe's face as she diligently built a humidity tent to help the mycelium along when they didn't sprout from water alone.

Something about her saying the mushrooms just needed a little more help. That same afternoon, she texted me a picture of a tiny little growth. A light brown tube growing out of the log, right near the top of the grape bag tent. So I dug out my email and messaged the clinic.

After I stupidly went and got us a stupid dog I now have to drive to daycare on my way to work.

I'M NOT EVEN sure how I'm going to survive meeting with the fertility doc. I actually don't even know if it's the same woman I saw the first time, when I stormed out of her office and (according to Chloe) flushed my marriage down the toilet.

Eventually I find the office and sign in on the computer in the waiting room. I'm startled when an assistant immediately pokes her head through the door and says, "Theodore? The doctor will see you now."

I swallow and nod, adjusting my tie as I follow her down the hall. She smiles and gestures for me to enter an office. I take a seat in the chair, unaccustomed already to sitting on the subordinate side of the desk in a room like this. This office isn't so different from mine...except this one has no windows or daylight and the art looks shitty. I sniff, wondering if it's obnoxious to be comparing office spaces.

I don't have to wait long before Dr. McClendon enters the room. "Ted! Nice to see you again."

"Is it?" The question is out of my mouth before I can stop it. I'm tense and on edge, my knee working up and down in a frenzy.

Dr. McClendon sighs and slides into her seat. "I know nobody *wants* to have to see me." She smiles without showing any teeth. "But I am glad that you decided to come back. I think you've got some good options here with us."

I add nervous finger tapping to the knee bounce and swallow. "You said I had low numbers..."

She nods. "That's right. And we might never know why that is. But there are things we can do about that. You could still father a child, Ted."

I feel a lump form in my throat. "But not the right way." I spit out the words as if it's my own father speaking. There was always a right way to do things...and anything else didn't count as far as he was concerned. I now recognize that mistakes on a farm could cost us an entire year of income, but the "one right way" approach to life runs deep in my veins. I don't know how to make sense of this sperm situation.

Dr. McClendon frowns. "I don't know that there is a *right* way to make a family. I can tell you that I believe we can take a sample or two from you, filter it and clean it, and get a nice group of motile sperm."

"Filter it?" My leg stops shaking as I imagine some sort of sieve on a condom.

Dr. McClendon nods. "We'll put the semen in a centrifuge, spin out the debris, and get a concentrated little pearl of the best swimmers." She snaps her fingers. "I do it every day."

"You personally spin semen?" I arch a brow at her, wondering what that looks like.

"Well, my lab staff do the spinning. But once they prepare it, I'd be the person to inject it."

My face contorts. "You put it back in my balls? The sperm pearl?"

Dr. McClendon winces. "Ted, I think we need to back up a few steps here." She folds her hands on the desk and leans forward. "At this point, we are looking at intrauterine injection as your best option to conceive." I open my mouth to say something else and she holds up a hand. "We will chart your wife's cycle and determine when she's ovulating. Then you'll both come in to the lab. You'll provide a sample, we'll clean it up like I said, and we'll inject it into..." She looks at her notes. "We'll inject it into Chloe's uterus."

I stare, trying to imagine my wife waiting on a hospital bed with her legs splayed open as I jack off, only to have Dr. McClendon impregnate her with a syringe of debris-free jizz. Dr. McClendon makes an empathetic face. "I know this isn't how you thought things would go. I promise, you're not alone here in this." I remember Chloe's teammate Dana saying she and her wife used a clinic to get pregnant. It must have been the same process.

I swallow. "And this works? All this stuff you described?"

She nods and scratches her chin. "We usually see conception after three attempts. Sometimes we can freeze your sample and blend it with a fresh one for a super-charged—"

"I can't jerk off in there three times," I interrupt. "Have you seen that room?"

The doctor clears her throat and leans back in her chair. "I can have the lab staff talk you through some other options in that regard. There really don't have to be barriers to success here."

Neither of us says anything for an uncomfortable stretch of time and I finally clutch the arms of my chair. "I'd like to find out what's wrong...what caused my...deficiency."

"We went through your personal history together, Ted. Sometimes these things just happen."

I stare at the wall. It'd be so much easier if there was a specific cause, something to blame. Too much soccer? Hot tubs? Nope. I just have faulty balls. I run my tongue along my teeth and cross my arms over my chest. "I need to think about this."

Dr. McClendon nods. "Of course. Take all the time you need." She slides me some papers. "Once you make a decision, we'll bring you and Chloe in together and plan next steps."

I nod and stand up, rolling the papers into my jacket pocket. I thank the doctor for her time and slink back through the halls, unsure if I'll tell Chloe about this conversation. How would I even begin?

I realize that even being here is more of the same thing I keep doing. I need to talk to Pam about why I get so deep in the planning process for Big Things before I even tell Chloe what's going on. She must have felt totally blindsided by the damn dog, by the house when we hadn't discussed moving. By all of it. WE never discussed moving. I thought about it, researched it, decided it was a good idea. Why in the hell didn't I rope her in on any of that?

I drag a hand through my hair and pull out my phone. I don't want to call her because I know she's irate about the dog.

Back at the house, said dog is delighted to see me. I squat down to greet him, forgetting that I'm still wearing nice slacks from work as he puts his paws all over my legs. It's been years since I've had a dog. I can't help but smile at the little guy. Farm dogs aren't really this sort of friendly. But then, I guess farm dogs have more to do all day.

"Do you need a job? Is that what you need?" He licks my hand a few times in response and I laugh, trying to imagine him running along beside a tractor or barking at the hay baler. "You'd get along with the chickens, I think. They wouldn't have been scared of you."

My parents raised chickens and soybeans. Nothing on this earth smells worse than chicken manure, but apparently it's the best fertilizer around if you want to avoid the chemical stuff. I would have learned more about it if I'd majored in agricultural science like Dad suggested. Since I was "going to do that whole college thing anyway."

I think about how my parents must have felt when I told them I'd gotten an athletic scholarship and would be leaving the state for college.

I assumed they knew I planned to go to college—why else would I get up early and stay up late to squeeze soccer in around farm chores? They acted like...well, they acted like Chloe did when I told her about the house...shocked, confused, and a little offended.

The dog barks, shaking me back to the present. He tears off down the hall and I follow him to Chloe's office, where I find him licking the shelves. "That's pretty weird, dude." I squat down to check if he has damaged anything. It seems like he's mostly lapping at some of her research volumes about colonial herbal medicine in Appalachia.

I take a look at the paperback on the desk, realizing I never finished reading it. I notice a line on the back cover encouraging me to buy the audiobook to listen along while I read, and so I scan the QR code to do that. A few minutes later, there's a man's voice in my ear buds, describing the thick, muscled thighs of Linus McClinton.

I glance at the dog, who is studying me intently. "Did you know about this?" He barks. "I'm not sure I'm ready for this," I tell him. "If I put this book by my bed, are you going to chew it? Please don't chew it, okay?"

I swear, the dog rolls his eyes at me.

"How about I change and we'll go throw a ball around. Does that sound good?" He yips and I laugh when he follows me up the stairs. I toss my suit into the basket I use for dry cleaning and see that the dog has jumped up onto the bed. He wags his entire body as he pulls my t-shirt around on top of the blankets.

"You little rascal! You better not put teeth marks in it." I tug very gently and he releases the shirt. No harm done. "Hm," I grunt. I pull out my phone.

> I'm sorry I sprung a dog on you

I type to Chloe.

> I should have paused when I didn't want to think of you alone in the house and asked you what you thought about that.

I walk out back with the dog and toss a tennis ball for him to fetch, laughing when it barely fits in his mouth. Eventually, I feel my phone vibrate with her response.

CHLOE PRESTON:

> Thank you for seeing my side.

19

CHLOE

THE MARRIAGE THERAPIST LOOKS PLEASED. "I notice you sat next to Teddy on the sofa today, Chloe. Would you care to talk about that?"

Pam is right. Teddy and I walked into her office yelling about the dog and I didn't even think about it. I just sat next to him. I look at him and shrug. "I was lost in conversation I guess."

Pam smiles from her perch on her kneeling stool. "Conversation is good."

Teddy grimaces and sighs. "I thought we'd come in here today and talk about the strides we made with the shiitake log." He quickly tells her about the humidity tent, making it sound like I did something much more exciting than dump grapes on a plate.

I like hearing him talk me up, even if I know he's about to bring up the dog. It reminds me of the way things used to be, when Teddy was excited about *me*.

Pam frowns. "But we're not talking about the strong response to a common task?"

I cross my arms over my chest and Teddy blows out a

breath. "I did something dumb again." I resist the urge to squeeze his leg encouragingly. What is with that? He went out and steamrolled this pet situation like he does everything else, and I'm feeling compelled to support him as he tattles on himself to our therapist!

I count my breaths as he tells her about the fur ball. Four beats in, and hold while he tells Pam he worried about me alone in the house. Four beats out and hold while he tells her he read that the sound of a pet in the house can deter potential burglars.

Pam leans forward. "So you moved directly from research into action? Is that right?" He nods and Pam whistles. She leans back and adjusts her notebook on her lap. "I'd like to back up and ask you to talk a bit more about your housing situation." Teddy opens his mouth to begin talking but Pam holds up a hand. "If I understand you correctly, your first home was a joint project. Much like the mushroom log, you worked together to troubleshoot and tackle the job."

She invites me to table any comments about the dog and I nod, gathering my thoughts about our house. Houses.

"That's fair." I turn to Teddy. "I guess you didn't need to look up how-to videos for all that because you already had that experience."

He grunts an affirmative sound. Teddy never likes to talk about farming or landscaping or any of the "hard man" stuff he did growing up. I frown. "What's with the grunts? I love that you know all that stuff, how to fix things."

I watch as his body tenses, as his shirt seems to grow more starch, feeding off his discomfort. Pam notices, too, and leans forward on her stool. "Teddy, can you tell us a little about your upbringing?"

He clenches his jaw uncomfortably and tugs at his

collar. "There was never enough of anything. Time, money, food. All of it was in short supply, and I was always expected to pull my weight."

"Pull weight. Are those your words?"

Teddy rolls his eyes and sighs. "No. That's pure Ronald Preston for you. There were never words of love or anything about being proud of me like Chloe had. Nobody had time for that."

Again, I resist the urge to reach for him, to comfort him. I'm not sure why. Of course I've heard this about his family before. I see it in person on the rare times we visit them, too. Life is austere in central Ohio. I've always wanted to shower him in affection. I suddenly remember years of him doing something big that used to seem helpful, and me responding with a rush of affection. I wriggle in my seat.

"Chloe," Pam interjects. "It seems like you have something to share?"

I nod. I turn sideways on the couch. "I was just thinking about your parents, of how they do seem so...tired isn't quite the right word. I was thinking how things are harsh where you grew up."

Teddy flexes his fingers and bunches them into fists again. "It wasn't easy leaving there to go to college. It wasn't easy staying away to get a desk job, either."

Pam nods. "I imagine your adult life feels very different in comparison." There's silence for a bit. I realize we've strayed away from talking about the house, which makes me anxious because I really do need to talk about that. Eventually Pam says, "Are you familiar with the hierarchy of needs?"

"Lord." Teddy scoffs and crosses his arms over his chest. His knee starts shaking, bouncing up and down.

"You sound skeptical?"

I run my tongue over my teeth, bracing myself. Teddy and I were in psychology together in college. He's definitely skeptical about all of it. I remind myself of this, of how much it says about him that he is sitting here with me in therapy anyway. I recall that he suggested therapy for us. I purse my lips and wait.

"It just all seems like excuses."

"Excuses for what?" Pam seems generally interested in this hot take on her field of expertise.

Teddy waves a hand. "Excuses for not getting shit done. For not sticking it out."

"Hm." Pam repositions herself again. "I'm hearing you talk about your parents sticking things out, even though it sounds like things were difficult. I also hear you say there wasn't much energy leftover for compassion or bonding. Is it fair to say your family used all of their energy seeing to basic needs—food, shelter, safety?"

"Yes. That's what I've been saying."

Pam smiles. "That's the bottom of the pyramid of human needs. Intimacy and a sense of belonging and achieve-ment...those needs are important, too."

Teddy throws his arms out. "That's what I've been trying to say. Belonging and achievement. That's why I bought the house, Chloe. I know it was wrong to cut you out of that conversation. I know that. But I needed..."

He drifts off and I stare, not sure what to say to him. "So the house signified achievement to you."

"Yes!" He sees me recoil a bit in surprise. "Yes," he says again, quieter.

Pam leans forward. "Chloe, I'm sensing that the house in the suburbs did *not* symbolize achievement for you?"

I shake my head. "I...I almost said I don't know what felt like an achievement before my books, but that's not true. It was an achievement for me to work on the house with Teddy. To stick with Teddy and build a life with him."

Pam nods and gestures for me to continue. "I was always sort of going with a flow. I never really had particular challenges or felt particularly passionate about anything. Until Teddy."

He faces me and swallows. I watch his throat move above that stiff collar and wish I could reach out and touch his warm skin.

"I went to college because I was supposed to. It's what people did in my family. I walked on the soccer team because I was good at it."

"You always looked so happy playing soccer," Teddy says, staring at the art on the walls again.

"I was happy playing soccer! It's fun." I shrug. "It's a game." He meets my eye again at that. I know it wasn't ever just a game to him. It was a means to an end—a scholarship, a rung on a ladder that got him somewhere he was going.

I wonder if he ever had a destination in mind or if it was always just "not here."

I reach for Teddy's hand and squeeze it, turning to Pam. "Early on, when Teddy finally worked up the nerve to tell me he liked me, I kept trying to go out and do fun things together. He wouldn't miss training or skip homework or do anything dangerous like climb trees to steal peaches." Teddy looks incredulous but I squeeze his hand again. "He always kept all that stuff in mind. School, our training...all of it. But he wanted to show me his favorite view on campus, and he promised we wouldn't even have to miss cardio to see it."

I remember the way the air felt in the stair wells as he ran up 36 flights of stairs with me huffing behind him, around and around to the top of the Cathedral of Learning

—a huge tower in the middle of the city with floor after floor of the university's classrooms and offices.

When we reached the top, heaving and panting and sweaty, it was twilight and Teddy stood behind me, watching the sun set over the city. I could hear my heart pounding in my ears and I could feel his heart pounding in his chest at my back. "Everything seemed possible then," I whisper. "We could see for miles, and everything was glowing orange in the sunlight and it all just seemed ours for the taking. And I felt like Teddy could help me get anywhere, that he knew the way."

Pam's eyes crinkle with her smile. "What happened then?"

Teddy grunts again. "I kissed the hell out of her."

I touch a finger to my lips, remembering the feel of him pressing me against the window, kissing me until our pulses synched. *What happens now* I asked him, and he grinned, taking my hand toward the door.

Now we run back down to the bottom, and do it all again.

20

TEDDY

I'M anxious to cook dinner with my wife. This is nuts.

My guilty conscience says I'm anxious to cook with her because I know she'll want to talk about hard shit. About all my shitty behaviors that got us here—with her living apart from me.

My heart races a little when I see a text from her.

Chloe Preston: Aren't you going to ask me about the nubbins?

I don't even pay attention during a meeting, trying to think of the perfect comeback. I don't want to mention the dog since that's a potential landmine. I thought I was done agonizing over flirt texts, and all I can come up with is a juvenile comparison between nubbins and genitalia. I eventually decide to play it straight.

> Please, my lovely wife, can you describe the nubbin progress on our fungus log?

CHLOE PRESTON:

> I love it when you talk about fungus.
> Remember when everyone on the men's team was passing athlete's foot around?

I grin. I'm not sure why this memory comes up for me as a pleasant one, but here I am—smiling at the vision of Chloe dragging me to the pharmacy for creams and sprays.

> Tough actin' Tinactin. You were pretty assertive about us both using it.

CHLOE PRESTON:

> I wasn't about to have fungus in our fancy apartment!

> And now you've got fungus in our house. On purpose!

CHLOE PRESTON:

> [mushroom emoji]

> Wait. We bought the psychedelic kind? You told me it was shiitake!

CHLOE PRESTON:

> Ha ha. I gotta run. See you soon!

> I can't wait.

I hope she knows how much I mean it.

I leave my office at exactly five and take off my tie as I walk to the car. I had meetings all day—in between text-flirting with my wife—and so I did something I don't love. I asked my assistant to go out and grab a bouquet of flowers for me. I figure it's more important to get to the house as quickly as I can, and I already have to swing by the dog place to get Rover Preston. I made sure to thank my admin profusely. It seemed like she thought the whole thing was sweet.

Here's hoping Chloe feels the same.

. . .

SHE FLINGS the front door open the second I put the SUV in park. She's brandishing a knife, but has a smile on her face so I feel like it's safe to approach the porch with the dog on a leash. He pees in the yard and she smiles at that, nodding. "It's time to harvest," she hollers. She's so cute, bouncing on her toes in the doorway. I notice that she dressed up a little. That's gotta be a good sign, right? Chloe is usually decked out in yoga pants and a baggy shirt.

Today she's wearing tight jeans and a less-baggy shirt. I stare at my wife's ass as she spins around and darts into the house, knife in front of her like a ceremonial baton in a parade. I follow quietly, snicking the door shut with my hip since my hands are full of flowers and suit jacket. I unclip the dog's leash and listen as his nails click on the floor while he explores. I hope he doesn't chew on anything, and I reach in my pocket for one of his toys. Chloe makes a bee-line for the mushroom log on the counter, not looking behind her to see that I've brought her a romantic bundle of grocery store dahlias.

I decide it doesn't matter, because she's got a huge grin on her face and I love seeing her happy like this. She seems like her old self right now: carefree and laughing. But she's also fixated on the task at hand. "I watched the video you sent, about how to harvest. Can I go first?"

"Go for it." As I say the words, she begins to work on the first mushroom.

Chloe spins the mushroom upside-down and shows me the gills. "I checked before I cut it. I knew this was going to be the one I picked first. Look at those white, fluffy rows."

"It looks perfect." I set the flowers down on the counter, unnoticed. I lean forward on my elbows, studying the log of mushrooms. I'd guess about six of them look ready to pick with a few more nubbins coming in from behind.

Chloe and I decided to make risotto with our harvest and she made a whole thing of going down to the special Italian grocer in the Strip District to buy the rice and chicken stock. Lots of people love that store, waiting in line for the fancy imported cheeses. The crowds always made me uncomfortable. It's been nice that Chloe is able to go during the week when it's less busy.

Rather than sit on that thought, I decide to take Pam's advice and offer up the compliment as soon as I think of it. "Hey." I place a hand on her shoulder and she turns to me. My breath catches at the sight of her beautiful face, so happy. Her eyes are pools of brown, and I can see the faint dusting of freckles on her nose. "I, um, just wanted to say I appreciate that you made the trip to Penn Mac for the dinner ingredients."

Her smile widens and I feel its warmth down to my toes. "It's not the same since the original cheese lady moved away."

I squeeze her shoulder. "I'm sure the parmesan is still delicious."

Chloe hands me the knife. "You should cut one, now, Bear."

I lean in close to her, our shoulders touching. I study the mushrooms, and I see which ones look ripe. But before I act, I make sure to ask her. "You think this one?" She nods and I slice into the stem, feeling the spongy fungus give way to the sharp knife edge. I spin it over in my hand and we both sigh at the sight of this perfect mushroom we grew together.

I laugh, thinking how absurd it is to be this excited about a lump of compost sprouting fungus.

"What's funny?"

I shake my head and cut another mushroom, gesturing first and waiting for her nod before slicing it free. Chloe and

I take turns until we are satisfied that we've gotten all the useable ones.

"All righty." She claps her hands. "Time to cook!"

"Hey, give me one second." I reach for the flowers and she tilts her head to the side.

"Have those been there this whole time?"

I grin. "You were so excited about your knife that you didn't even see me bring them in."

Chloe gathers them up and gives them a sniff, even though dahlias don't have a smell. I like how the deep reds and oranges look near her hair and brown eyes. I reach out a hand and stroke her cheek and appreciate the tingle of energy as she leans in to my touch. "They're beautiful, Teddy."

"Petals for my petal." The line is super cheesy, but she definitely appreciates it. Her smile widens and I watch as she shimmies her shoulders, savoring the flowers in her arms.

Smiling, Chloe grabs a water glass and wedges the flowers inside. "Who needs a vase, right?"

"I can bring a vase next time..."

The dog clicks into the kitchen and I realize I should get him a dish of water. I lean past Chloe and grab one of her cereal bowls, setting it on the floor near the doorway.

She shakes her head and gestures at the counter. "We should get started."

We stand side by side, chopping shallots and the mushrooms, while she tells me about the release strategy for her next book. 'Release strategy' is a phrase I'm familiar with from business school and I'm surprised to learn about the business concepts Chloe is applying to her work. I scratch my nose with the heel of the knife and she swats me in the arm. "You're going to cut yourself doing that."

"I'll cut myself worse if you hit me while I have a knife!" She laughs a little and I continue chopping. "I guess I didn't realize you had a marketing strategy."

She makes a face at me. "Well, yeah. How else do you think I sell books?"

"Sure, sure. I just hadn't stopped to think about the business side of it. Will you tell me more?"

I listen, flabbergasted, as Chloe describes her six-month plan to reach readers with ads, giveaways, how she's coordinating with other authors to promote each other's books in their newsletters. It would seem Chloe has earned the equivalent of my MBA degree from her office, just pecking away at things and asking other authors questions.

"This is amazing, babe. What sort of ROI do you get on your ads?"

She shrugs. "That's the part I'm still figuring out. Understanding which things work."

I sigh. "That seems like a pretty important piece of the enterprise."

Chloe reaches for the cutting board where I've chopped the shallots. She tilts them into the pot with the melted butter and rice and we both inhale at the explosion of aroma. "I'm working on it," she mutters. I lean against the counter as she stirs in the first round of broth.

The dog circles our feet a few times, wagging his entire fluffy body. Chloe massages his head with her toe inside her sock. She bites her lip and looks at me.

Now comes the part I was anxious about: standing around, stirring risotto slowly, pouring in liquid drop by drop as we inevitably talk about our Hard Shit.

Chloe scrapes at the bottom of the pot with the wooden spoon, not looking up at me as she says, "I think we should both get a chance to talk about where we'd like to live, long-term, and *why.*"

"Sure. Yes. Of course. But also, I'm just really impressed that you're doing a lot of the stuff I learned in grad school, without actually having gone to grad school for that. You know?"

She takes a breath and stirs the rice. I nod, recognizing that we are going to move away from this topic.

"You know I chose the city on purpose, right? You remember that?" I nod again. "I chose an urban college and I just really like living close to people, close to all different things like soccer facilities and quirky Italian markets and plant stores that carry shiitake kits."

I hear her. For Chloe, the city means connection and curiosity. I let her words sink in and try to pinpoint what felt so alluring to me about the suburbs. She hands me the spoon and I take over at the stove, stirring a bit and adding a little more liquid. I tap on my chest. "I know that money isn't everything, but it sure feels that way to me, Chloe. Sometimes I worry I still smell like a farmer. I look down and worry the grease and dirt will still be etched into the cuts on my fingers from fixing machines." I hold my hands out in front of me.

Chloe traces a finger along the back of one of my hands and a shiver runs down my spine. I always want her so badly, but it's been so long now I don't know what to do about this lust she just triggered. "Nobody can take your degrees from you, Teddy. Your education isn't going anywhere."

I bob my head in agreement. "Pam said the new house is a symbol of wealth and prosperity for me."

"I remember. What do you think?"

I shrug. "She's probably right. But Chloe, it's a really nice house. Isn't it?"

She frowns. "It's hard for me to be objective about it."

I nod and continue stirring the risotto. I peer into the pot and scoop out a few grains of rice with the spoon. "I think this might be about ready."

She smiles and slides the butter dish closer to me. I start scooping in the butter as Chloe grates the cheese and a few minutes later, the two of us are hunched over the pan, staring at the creamy, savory dish we made together. I watch her scoop a steaming portion into one of the mismatched bowls and I'm touched when she slides it toward me, moving on to scoop herself some of the food.

"Hey, Chloe." There's a lump in my throat and I close my eyes. "The house is nothing without you in it."

"Thank you for saying that." She smiles and holds out a spoon. I accept it from her and we walk around the counter to enjoy our meal.

21

CHLOE

IT's surreal to be living separate from Teddy. I have to talk to him about something and, in order to do so, I have to call him on the phone.

It's Teddy, for god's sake. I've been with Teddy ever since that day in the training room, when his teammate told me Teddy was crushing on me and I invited him to ice ankles together.

We just clicked then. I wish we were clicking now. I know that whatever changed with us...happened before the fertility clinic. I just wish it were easier to figure out what the problem really is.

I take a deep breath and pull him up in my phone. He's still number one in my favorites, my in case of emergency person. I mean, he's still my husband.

"Chloe?"

"Hey."

There's silence for a bit before he asks, "Everything okay?"

"What? Oh. Yes. I, um, well...my parents are expecting us for Thanksgiving."

"Oh."

"Yeah." I scrape at a tiny drop of paint on the window sill, irritated that it's there, irritated that Teddy would have remembered drop cloths and been more thorough about the tape, just in case. But then I remember that it's easier to scrape off one drop of paint than spend hours taping. "I'd like you to come along still, if you're interested." I sigh. "We could talk in the car, you know?"

"I'd like that, babe. Where would we stay?"

Another landmine. "The apartment." My parents have a tiny finished space above the garage for when my brother and I come home. Chris and I take turns using it if we're both home at the same time, the other sibling relegated to their childhood bed along with their spouse. "At least we get the bigger bed, right?"

"Yeah." Teddy chuckles. Chris and his spouse are both six-foot something, and they're still in that new phase of romance where they cram together in a twin bed rather than part overnight in separate rooms.

"I could offer to trade him. But he'd want to know why..." I haven't talked to my parents about our separation. I've been deflecting their questions about grandchildren and my career, too. They do know I'm publishing romance novels under a pen name, but not much else.

"I'm not really up to getting into all that with them, if that's okay with you." He groans. "I don't want to ask you to keep more secrets. I know that goes against our agreement with Pam. If we could just avoid bringing it up that—"

"I don't want to talk about us to my family," I interject. "We're on the same page there."

"Well. Good. Okay." A long pause. "You think it's okay to bring the dog?"

I feel my breath catch. "I forgot about the dog."

Teddy sighs. "I've been calling him Rover for now."

I wince at that. "We can do better than that, I think."

"We?" His voice sounds so hopeful. I guess I am subconsciously attached to the dog by now.

We haven't talked much since we made dinner together and finished our mushroom-growing project. It's like we need a tangible to-do list in order to be around each other. "I'll double-check with my parents, but we have to come up with a better name by the time we get there."

"I'll make a list." He says this with excitement, and I know lists do energize him.

"Sounds good." I chip away at the paint dot, not quite ready to hang up.

"You doing okay?"

"I finished painting. I've been proofing my audio for the new release, so I've had a lot of hours to fill."

"What does that mean? Proofing audio?"

"Oh." I pace around the living room and explain how the audio production company sends me my files, all prettied up and scrubbed and I listen through to make sure the narrator actually read what was on the page.

"How can you listen like that and paint at the same time? Don't you have to read along?"

"Nah." I grin. "I guess I give them some benefit of the doubt, but I know my work pretty well. I can tell if something sounds off and then I just pull up the file and check."

"It's blowing my mind that you do all that."

"Yep. I do a lot." I freeze, because I think my response was defensive, but then maybe his comment was a little dismissive. Or something.

Teddy obviously is having feelings about his remark, too,

because he hastens to add, "That came out wrong. I want to offer a compliment, Chloe. I'm so bad at this."

"Well, I like compliments..." I bite my lip, waiting as he sorts through his thoughts.

"Okay. So I think it's really impressive that you're producing your work in different formats, and that you're the project manager for all of them. We have different team leads here for different products, you know?"

"I don't know. I still don't understand what your company does." We both laugh at that, because I used to work there. It's been a joke between us for a long time, that I never really understood the mission statement. "Thank you for the compliment, Teddy."

"You're welcome, love."

"I'll pick you up Wednesday morning since you're on the way."

"Sounds good."

It's on the tip of my tongue to say "love you, bye," or something, but I don't let the words flow. Instead we just hang up.

A FEW DAYS LATER, I pull into a driveway I own, and don't know whether I should get out, whether I should use my garage door opener. I'm grateful I don't have to spend a long time worrying about it because Teddy and the dog shoot out the front door swinging, like they were waiting for me to get here. I like the idea of that, of him antsy and excited to see me, even if it's not about me so much as it's about his worry about lateness in general. Teddy hates keeping people waiting.

He heaves a dog crate and a fluffy bed into the hatch and tosses his duffel in the back seat. I watch in the rearview mirror as he clips the dog into some sort of harness.

"Hey." I catch a whiff of Teddy as he slips into the passenger seat and I'm momentarily frozen by lust. He smells like he always does. It's just that I'm not immune to it, maybe, or his scent had drifted into my subconscious. Whatever is going on, I'm flooded with deodorant and laundry detergent and pheromones as eau de Teddy wafts around my electric car. "You okay?" His brow furrows in concern and I realize I must be staring. I close my mouth, which had been hanging open.

I decide to be honest with him. "You smell really nice, Ted." He blushes and smiles, settling in to his seat and looking at me.

"Did you pre-heat my seat for me?" I shrug. His smile widens. "Thank you."

I pull out of the subdivision and turn onto the highway, heading north toward New York State and the small, lake-side college town where I grew up. Teddy pulls out his phone and I glance over to see he has opened his notes app.

"I know we still need to name the dog, but can we talk through the plan real quick?" I realize this is something I could list to Pam as a compromise we've already made. Whereas I know and understand that my family will never sway from holiday traditions and, thus, know the routine down pat, Teddy needs to discuss each step each year. It feels like a compromise that I go over the routine with him, that I want him to feel comfortable in this way even if it's been a decade and he should know the drill by now.

"You got it. So as soon as we cross state lines..."

He grins. "We can purchase alcohol at rest stops." We share a laugh. I've lived with him in Pennsylvania since college, which means I'm 12 years into the state's restrictive policies about alcohol, and I'm still upset about it. "You'll fuel up and I'll grab the vino. Oh. Wait. Your car doesn't do gas."

"Huh." I glance at him. "I guess we usually take yours."

"Let me check if our stop has a charging station." We learn that our preferred rest stop doesn't have a place for me to top off my electric vehicle. This sends Teddy down a wormhole making lists of all the possible spots for us to charge up while we're staying in my hometown for the weekend, while I subconsciously acknowledge the benefit in going over the routine out loud.

"Glad we talked through it," I tell him, smiling as he drops pins on the map app on his phone.

"Mm hm." He taps around a few more times. "Okay, so then this evening...you're making stuffing with your mom?"

"And dad will drag you, Chris, and Denver through feats of strength and errands."

Teddy rolls his eyes. "I still don't see why we all have to go to all the stores for the pies and groceries. If it were you and me, we'd divide and conquer."

"We would." I nod. "But Chris does like to compete with you about the wood chopping."

"Think how much more wood we could chop if we drove separately for the errands and all met back at the stump!"

I swat at his shoulder, both of us fully aware that my dad will never willingly part from tradition.

I grin and clutch the wheel a little tighter. "What about Taki for the dog? Like shiitake?"

Teddy frowns and shakes his head. "No. That's not the name."

We bicker over traditional dog names, human names that sound funny—Teddy quickly vetoes Alfred and I laugh out loud at Roland. We cross into New York and Teddy navigates to the new Preston Preferred rest stop. I get the car plugged in and stand with the leash while not-Roland does his business in the grass.

Teddy emerges from the store with more wine than the six of us could ever drink this weekend. "They sell it by the box here." He delights in showing me the increased selection compared to the store we usually visit. "We could call him Vino? Vinny?"

"Nope." The three of us climb back inside the car to wait. Teddy's and my fingers brush against each other's as we both cuddle the pup. I chew on the inside of my cheek.

I like this, sitting with him in the quiet, chilly car, trapped while we wait for the charge. He stashes the wine behind my seat and then turns his body to face mine. "Will you tell me more about your marketing challenges?" He blushes again and swallows slowly. "I looked you up a little bit and it seems fair to say you sell quite a few books...but you said you aren't sure which promotions move the needle."

I nod and tuck my hair behind my ears. "Even though I've only got two books out, I seem to have found a sweet spot in the market."

"What does that mean, quantitatively?"

I roll my lips between my teeth and reach for my purse. "It might be easier to just show you." I pull out my phone and open the app for my business bank account. He scoots the dog to the side and then tilts his head close to mine and makes a strangled sound when he sees the balance in my checking account.

"Christ, Chloe, you cannot just keep that much cash in a checking account. What are you thinking?"

I shrink away from him. The dog yelps. "I was planning to get a tax helper. I just keep getting side tracked."

"A tax helper? Oh, godddd you don't have an accountant? You've got six figures of cash?" I nod. His eyes bulge. "How long has this been? The royalties like this?"

I squint, trying to remember when I had the viral social media video that really brought readers in to my *Redcoat* book. "A year? Maybe a little less."

Teddy tugs at his shirt collar. "Chloe, you didn't tell me any of this when I filed our taxes this year."

I cross my arms over my chest. "Well, you didn't ask!"

"You can't just not file income taxes because you're upset with me and my communication shortcomings." He fans himself with his hands and rests his head against the dog's back. "I'm going to have a stroke." I watch as the furry guy licks Teddy's face, trying to calm him down I guess.

"Some months my ad spend was higher than my royalties," I snap at him. And then I roll my eyes, realizing how I sound. "I told you, it's on my to-do list to get a tax helper." I start feeling guilty about the secret house money from my dad. I'm sure I owe taxes on that, too.

Teddy pokes his fingertips into his temples, making tight circles as he breathes. "Babe. You're going to have to pay a penalty. You're supposed to file quarterly when you're self-employed."

"I know that!" I'm shouting now and we're fogging up the windows as we argue. "I had my house history business, remember?"

He nods. "And that's why I don't understand why you didn't clarify to me that when you stopped the house history work, you were replacing it with other, vastly more lucrative work. Ohhh, god, my heart is racing."

"Honestly, Teddy, this is my problem. You don't need to worry like this."

"We are married, Chloe. Your problems are my problems."

"Oh, really? Just like your balls are my problem, too? Because you were real quick to punt that to me!"

He sits up and glares at me, shakes his head a few times, and then gets out of the car. I watch as he strides away and stands by the highway, hands in his pockets, glaring at the passing cars.

22

TEDDY

THWACK!

I FORGOT how damn good it feels to swing an axe through a log. The second we pulled into the driveway at Chloe's parents' house, I slipped out of the silent car and headed for the wood pile out back. For years, I've been chopping wood here the hard way because Chloe's father prefers it, but today I'm going back to my roots.

I grab a log and lean it against another log and swing the axe overhead, splitting it in half with one swing to the long edge, and then two more rapid swings to get it into manageable chunks for the living room fireplace.

Thwack! Thwack-thwack.

The stack of logs is almost knee high by the time I hear Chloe's dad clucking his tongue at me. "Never saw anyone go about it that way." He stands next to me with his arms crossed, placing one boot on the axe head so it drops to the ground from my hand.

I pause to wipe the sweat off my forehead and shrug.

"This isn't TikTok. I was going for efficiency rather than sex appeal."

Robert Evers tilts his head as I reach for another log. "Why aren't you standing them up on the cuttin' stump like usual?"

I blow out a breath and look around, wishing I had a glass of water. "The logs aren't always sliced evenly," I explain. "It's not always stable to chop them standing vertically."

Robert nods, contemplating. "Show me your way again."

He nudges the axe with his boot and backs up. I grab a log, prop it diagonally on another log, and split it along the side with a grunt. Robert watches as I finish chopping the log into quarters and he reaches for the axe once I'm done.

I set up the next log for him and stand out of the way as he chops the wood, his face shifting in delighted surprise when he splits the log in one swing. He looks at me for a few beats. "You never said you knew a better way to split logs."

I scratch my neck, wishing again for the water. "I wanted you to like me." I consider my motives further and add, "I wanted you to root for me. With Chloe."

He waves a hand. "Aw, hell, Ted, she's been a goner for you for a long time." He stares up at the sky like he's trying to gauge the time. "I got Chris and Denver all ready to head out on our errands. Normally we do that before the wood, but I guess you know that."

I take a deep breath. "If it's all the same to you, Rob, I'm not really up to the crowds at the bakery and stuff."

He stares at me, like I just suggested we skip Thanksgiving dinner in favor of takeout pizza. I look over his shoulder and see Chloe's brother and his spouse waving from the driveway. They're both playing with the dog while Chloe stands to the side not making eye contact with me.

Denver drapes their arm around Chris's waist and hollers, "Are we switching the routine? I'm not dressed for chopping yet."

Robert shakes his head. "Ted here needs some time alone!" He sighs and looks up at the house before adding, more quietly, "Chloe mentioned you've been under some stress lately. She and Karen already got going on the stuffing."

I observe Robert's obvious distress at the notion of swaying from tradition, from the expected order of operations for this holiday. I wonder if this is how Chloe sees my fastidiousness, like an extension of her parents and their rigid approach to, well, everything. I know Chloe goes out of her way to never contradict her father, or express discontent with his ideas. I don't want her to bring that attitude into our marriage.

I think about Robert's confusion that I've always known another way to chop the wood and never bothered to mention it to him for fear of rocking the boat. It's easy to see how Chloe viewed a lot of my actions in the same light. I really thought all this distance began at the fertility clinic, but I'm starting to see we've been coming to a boil for a long time. Before I got my MBA. Maybe even before she got laid off. It just became a habit I guess, hiding part of herself from me when my misconception seemed good enough.

I nod at Rob. "I'd like to stay here and get the dog situated. I'll save some energy to chop more with you three when you're back."

"That'll work, though I'll miss your keen eye for finding parking at the Wegman's."

I grin and line up another log. "I'm sure Chris and Den can help you out, Robert." He takes off and I stack another dozen or so split logs before I feel more in control of my emotions.

Objectively, Chloe has a tax liability problem and she needs support in solving it. Objectively, this impacts both of us. I don't even know if she's set up as an LLC or if she's operating as herself, tax-wise. I need to find a way to discuss this with her that doesn't morph into her yelling at me about my balls.

My clothes are clinging to me with sweat despite the November chill and I head up to the apartment above the garage, hoping to shower and change before I tackle even more chopping with Chloe's family later. I walk into the warm apartment and make a bee line for the kitchen sink, stripping my shirt on the way and dropping it to the floor as I put my mouth directly around the tap.

Once I no longer feel like I'm parched, I reach for a glass and try to drink a little more civilly. I don't notice my wife walk into the room until I'm groaning into my second glass of water. I look at her through the distorted bottom of the vessel and she's still stunning viewed through thick glass, her chestnut hair shimmering in the afternoon sun through the window.

Chloe smiles and leans against the counter beside me. "I came to check on you."

I set the glass on the counter and reach for her hair. I've always loved it, loved running my fingers through it, wrapping it around my wrist and giving it a tug when we're feeling frisky. It's been ages since we did anything like that.

I watch her breath catch as my fingers trace through her ponytail, spreading her hair along her chest. My hand is dirty from the logs, sweaty from the work. The contrast reminds me of how I've always felt about our pairing. Me, a crusty farm boy from Ohio lusting after the most pristine, most beautiful woman I'd ever seen.

"Where's Yippy?"

She rolls her eyes. "That's not his name." Her voice is a whisper. "He's inside with my mom."

Chloe's chest rises and falls as I stroke her hair, trying not to think about her tax debt or the way I'm fixating on it instead of the fact that my wife launched a six-figure author career and I failed to notice. She licks her lip and her voice shakes as she says, "You smell like sweat now. But I still like it."

I grin and tug her closer to me, my other hand wrapping around her waist. I'm probably leaving dirt streaks on her clean shirt. I lean in close and take a long whiff of my wife. "You smell like onions. I like that, too."

She swallows and drops a hand to my shoulder, her finger tracing a path along my collarbone. How long has it been since we touched one another? Since I held her? I wince, remembering the night at the hotel. My skin aches for her. I remember the early days of our relationship, when I could never find the right words to tell her how I felt, so I'd try to tell her through my touch. Tried to worship her body with my tongue, on my knees at her feet.

Chloe takes a step closer to me, her legs pressing into mine ever so slightly, her boobs making contact with my chest through her soft sweater. The sunlight dances in her eyes as she looks up at me. She draws a ragged breath. "Teddy." I recognize the need in her voice, the wanting, and even though it feels as scary as the very first time, I lean forward and claim her mouth with mine.

She melts into me with a groan that I feel through my entire body. Chloe's hands skate along my back, nails dragging sparks along my skin. I'm still barely touching her except with my mouth, but I correct this quickly, wrapping that hair tightly around my wrist and tilting her head, exposing her throat and running my tongue up the column of her neck from her collar to the tip of her chin.

"Oh, fuck, Teddy. You're always so god damned hot." I back her up against the counter, rocking my hips against her as I nip at her lower lip. Everything feels like the first time, except her body is beautifully familiar to me because she's been mine for so long.

"Take your shirt off," I tell her. I grip the edge of the counter on either side of her, meeting her eyes as she strips. "Bra, too." Chloe nods and reaches behind her back to unhook the plain, black cotton. Soon, she's standing topless in front of me, her beautiful breasts punctuated by deep rose nipples. I reach up to cup them in my hands, thumbs skating along the pointed peaks. She groans and I nod, approvingly. "Beautiful," I whisper, and I drop my head to kiss each rosy nub.

Chloe starts to sag and I heft her up onto the edge of the counter, wishing I'd leaned in to her arms from the first hint of upset. This is how we come together, she and I. How could I let it go this long? I kiss her mouth again, my tongue clashing with hers as she winds her arms around my neck. I love the feel of our skin pressed together, my sweat the only thing between us.

I grunt when Chloe slips a hand down to my crotch, and my hips jut into her palm. "Ooh, Teddy, yes, please." She opens her thighs wider, her feet digging into my ass as she tries to pull me closer to her center.

I can't remember why we've had such distance between us, why things have been so difficult. All we need is this—friction and heat and thrusting, head-clearing release. I fumble with the top of Chloe's jeans, hearing the zipper creak open to give me enough space to slide my hand inside her pants. Her delighted moan eggs me on and I chuckle when I feel her teeth against the skin of my chest.

I manage to get one finger inside my wife, feeling her hot and wet all around me. I moan at the sensation, at the perfect tightness I've missed for so long. "Fill me up, Teddy," she breathes. "Please. Fill me up."

Chloe lifts her hips and starts yanking down her jeans, grunting with the effort. But her words have a terrible impact. Fill her—I can't, can I? Not really. My heart races as I realize the truth of it all. I can't fill her with a baby. I can only fill her bank account, and she doesn't even need that from me anymore. I step back, away from Chloe, shaking my head.

She doesn't need me.

"Teddy." Her eyes plead and her body begins to tremble. "Teddy, I meant with your cock. I—"

I back away farther, dragging a palm down my face. "We shouldn't have done this without talking first."

Chloe's cheeks redden and I see her sag, trying to cover her nakedness. She feels exposed now. I bend down and grab her shirt, holding it out for her. "I should shower."

Her jaw works up and down and she makes a crying sound. In what's become a habit for me, I walk away, leaving my wife spread open and confused, empty.

23

TEDDY

I DON'T JERK off in the shower today. Lately, that's become my private shame ritual, touching myself to visions of my horny wife. Today, when I could have had the real thing, I fell apart. This can't continue.

I rinse myself off and wonder what our therapist would say. What my father would say. What the guys from my college soccer team would say. I come up empty.

BY THE TIME I emerge dressed in flannel, Chloe is nowhere in sight. I head into the main house and find the family getting ready for pre-Thanksgiving dinner. Rob and crew are back from marketing and they all glance up at me, pausing in their process of passing out wine and beer bottles.

"Get you a drink, Ted?" Chloe's father holds a bottle of white in one hand and one of the boxed reds we brought in the other.

I gesture at the red and nod my head in thanks as we all

sit down. There's an awkward silence I don't think I'm imagining. Even the dog is quiet as he wags his tail from his dog bed a few feet away from the table. Between my out-of-sequence wood chopping and my refusal to go on the family errands, I know they can tell something is amiss. I also suspect Chloe wouldn't have told them anything substantive.

Denver dishes out salad and makes eye contact with my brother-in-law. They clear their throat. "So, Chris and I have news."

Chloe leans on her elbows, her face eager to hear. Chris rips off a hunk of bread and passes the basket along the table. "Yep. Den and I signed up to be foster parents."

There's a chorus of delight around the table as they explain how they read about the high number of teens and older kids who need a safe place to stay both short and long-term. Denver shrugs. "We figure we've got the room. I know we can't make special requests or whatever, but our agency knows we are particularly open to fostering queer kids."

Chloe's dad takes a deep breath. "Now, I thought that word was a slur."

Chris shakes his head. "It depends who is using it and how, but Den just means we're here for kids of all sexualities and gender expression. Or exploration." Chris winks at Den, who blushes behind the pepper grinder. I chuckle because they're both being cute.

Chloe reaches for her brother's hand and squeezes it. "This is amazing news. I love that you're doing this."

"Thanks, sis." The family talks about logistics—where will the kids go to school and will Denver and Chris have to figure out childcare. It all sounds extremely complicated, but it also sounds like they've thought through all of it, together. I can't help but compare their team approach here to whatever it is Chloe and I have been sifting through the past few years. Den and Chris seem like they're on exactly the same page.

Denver's upbringing wasn't much different from mine, and being non-binary added a layer of complication to their family dynamics. So why am I a ball of panicked rash decisions and they're able to clearly talk shit out with their spouse to the point that they already know which of them can take parental leave to help with the adjustment of a foster child at home?

I remain silent for most of the meal, springing up to help clear the dishes the second Chloe's dad begins to pat his stomach and lean back in his chair. He drapes an arm around his wife and looks between the kids. "Lots to be thankful for this year."

I start scraping plates into the compost pail and rinsing the dishes, hoping they'll forget I'm here, knowing I should pull Chloe aside and talk to her.

"Who's ready to stack some firewood?" Rob stands up and stretches as Denver and Chris reach for their boots by the back door.

"I'll be out in a few," I say, gesturing to the sink. Rob makes a face and slides open the back door. Chloe lingers behind and her mother makes herself scarce. She grabs the dog's leash and they all go outside, blessedly giving me a minute alone with my wife.

She leans on the counter opposite me, watching as I rinse a few more plates. I take a deep breath and close my eyes. "I went back to the clinic and saw Dr. McClendon."

Chloe gasps. "When?"

I shrug. "I forget. Not too long ago. She said we have some options." Chloe's eyes tear up and she bites her lip, so I explain to her about the sperm spinning.

She takes a deep breath. "Teddy, I think we have some work to do before we try something like that."

I nod. "I wanted you to know I went to the clinic. That I'm open to conversation about it."

"Thank you. I want to be in on these aspects of your life. Of our life."

"I know that. Rationally I know that." I set the last plate in the dishwasher and stoop to add the soap and turn it on. I should walk around the counter and sit next to her for this conversation but there's something soothing about the expanse of granite between us. I lean on the edge.

"You have to let me in, Teddy."

I sigh. "I was listening to Denver, thinking about how they grew up. They don't seem to panic about their life plan or whatever."

"I don't care about Denver right now, though. I care about you."

She reaches for my hand and I hold it, stretched across the sink. Our arms form a bridge, a little like the art in Pam's office. "I'm afraid that I'll wind up with nothing. Broke, starving, having to put on roofs in the fucking summer just to keep one over my own head." She nods. "I'm afraid you'll leave me and I'll be alone."

Chloe closes her eyes. "Teddy, I have left you. I left."

I nod. "How can I get you to come back?" She squeezes my hand again and shrugs. "Should I sell the house? I can sell the house."

"Please do." Chloe's response is immediate, without any hesitation. Much the same as my pull to buy it in the first place. I cringe. And then I realize something.

"So you want me with you in the Highland Park house?"

Chloe lets go of my hand. "I don't know right now." I blow out a breath and lean forward, knuckles digging into the granite. She winces and takes a deep breath. "I should tell you something, too." I nod and she curls her lips in before blurting, "My dad did give me that downpayment money. For the first house. He put it in a trust or something and I've ignored it."

I feel like she just kicked me in the balls with that information. It meant so much to me that we got that house on our own, that we found the right loan and made the payments ourselves. I bunch my hands into fists, squeeze them a few times, and release them. The door slides open and Chloe's brother pokes his head inside. "Ted, we need you to show us the technique again. Dad's fixated on efficiency all of a sudden."

"Be right there," I say, not looking away from my wife. I hear the door slide shut. "Chloe, you're important to me. You're the most important thing to me. I want to figure out all my other shit, you know?" She nods her head and bites her lip again. "But we also need to talk about you. You've got this entire amazing career *and* it's a tax liability. And we absolutely need transparency with our finances. This cannot be optional."

Chloe's eyes fly open and I hold up a hand. "What I mean is that you've got a great thing going and...I had no idea. And I want to be there with you to celebrate. That's what I mean."

She starts crying and I actually do rush around the counter and put an arm around her. "I kept you in the dark," she says. I nod, because it's true, even if I'm the one who pulled the electricity on that communication.

"I'm going to go swing an axe with your dad and your brother now. You wanna watch?"

This gets a little laugh out of her and we walk outside together. "What about Beave? Like eager beaver." I point to the dog, who is yipping and dashing back and forth between Robert, Chris and Denver.

Chloe shakes her head but squeezes my hand before stooping to pick up the dog and hold him safely out of the path of the axe.

24

CHLOE

FROM THE LOOKS of this Foof meeting, everyone had a little too much bonding time with their extended families over Thanksgiving. Even the Stag women seem sick of each other, and that family is notoriously close-knit. I've never seen folks this spread out at Bridges and Bitters. Must be something going around.

Esther, who normally would have a tray of new concoctions for us, saunters into the room with a bottle of whiskey dangling from one hand and a tray of shot glasses in the other. Orla Brady nods approvingly. Her family drinks a lot of Irish whisky.

Samantha Vine pounds her empty glass on the table, the sharp clunking sound a signal for everyone to hush their murmur and get started. "What's everyone been up to this past week? I had to deal with my siblings for three days, so it's someone else's turn to talk."

She arches a brow at me and I take a deep breath, swallowing the whiskey for liquid courage. Samantha dangles the power stick at me, but I shake my head. "Most of you know Teddy and I are going through a rough patch." I stare into the mouth of the glass when I say it but I can feel everyone's nods of encouragement to continue. "We had a series of weird fights the entire weekend and I think I realized something."

"Realizations are great!" Logan Brady raises her glass to me in salute before taking a tiny sip of her drink.

I nod. "It's not easy to say this stuff, though."

"We're here for you." Piper pats my leg. I squeeze her hand and think about how brave she was at the last meeting, sharing her business plan and her leap to self-employment. It's much more of a risk for Piper, who doesn't have a spouse at home pulling in an executive salary while she branches out. If she can do that, I can probably face what I've been fretting over.

"I hid my career from Teddy. It wasn't just that he didn't ask about it—which he didn't." Sam makes a disapproving sound. "But I deliberately hid things, I think. I didn't ask him for input when I stopped doing the house histories. I didn't shout it from the rooftops when my first book hit the best-seller list."

Esther rolls her eyes. "You barely told *us* about it. Thankfully Sam reads those newspapers every morning and saw you in there!"

I wince and lean back in my chair. "Why do I do these things? Why am I like this?"

Piper frowns and taps her fingers on the table. "Am I remembering that you don't like to rock the boat with your parents? Didn't you say that?"

I shrug. "Doesn't everyone feel like that, though? Who wants to piss off their parents?"

Piper nods. "Yeah, but I think—and this is just a hunch—but maybe you got used to being the good kid and always sort of went with the flow."

I think about her phrase "go with the flow." That's always how I describe myself. I never really had a preference for my position in soccer—just went with wherever coach needed me. I didn't have a particular passion for the work we were doing when Teddy and I applied for Hoster Corp after college. But it seemed like a good enough opportunity and it meant I was close with my Teddy Bear.

I shake my head. "I don't know, Pipes. I think I'm just easygoing."

The conversation drifts to hiring freezes and how to recruit more women in male-dominated career fields, but I can't shake Piper's observation. Maybe it's true that I don't buck the current with my family, but that's usually in response to things that don't matter much in the long run. Who actually cares where we go out to eat or what store we buy the Thanksgiving rolls from? I mean, my dad cares. And I don't. So how is that related to me keeping my career highlight reel from Teddy?

WHEN I GET HOME, the house feels too quiet. Too empty. Even the living room nest feels too sparse. I climb into the cot and turn off most of the lights to try and create a sense of cozy cocoon, but I can hear each creak echo off the empty walls. I'm alone here with my thoughts and I don't like it.

I could call Teddy. He'd talk to me until I felt better. He'd probably drive down here if I asked him to. But I shouldn't ask him to until I mean it. "He'd probably leave the dog here with me," I mutter, tugging my sleeping bag closer around my ears.

I think again about Piper's observation and decide to call my brother. When he answers, though, I can't figure out how to drive in to that conversation. I stall. "Any word on the foster stuff?"

He laughs. "Oh, man, Chloe. Our social worker said we could have a kid here tomorrow if we complete the home visit. Tomorrow! Can you imagine?"

"Wow. There must be a lot of kids."

"So many. Den and I keep thinking we're not ready and we need to wait for the new year and all that but...I mean, if there's kids who need us..."

"It sounds like the Chris-Den is ready for expansion."

He giggles. "I told you, that nickname stinks. It's weird and it doesn't even work."

"Den is a noun. Chris is the adjective. Chris Den. Den of Chrises. I'm a writer so I get to be the expert."

He laughs louder this time. "Look at you being assertive for once." His tone is a little harsh behind the laughter.

"What's that supposed to mean?"

There's a pause. "I just don't think I've ever heard you assert expertise about something. For a second I thought maybe soccer, but I really don't think so."

"What do I need to be an expert about for soccer?"

"Chlo!" Chris snorts and I can hear him walking around his house. "You were a four-year starter on a D-1 team that went to nationals a few times. And you backed down in an argument with the neighbors about whether soccer is a phase in the U.S."

I huff. "It could be a phase..."

"A phase? Come on, Chloe."

I'm not sure why this conversation packs such a sting, but I don't like the direction it's taking. I take a deep breath. "Well I really just called to see how you were doing with the whole foster thing."

"We're doing great, sis. What's up with you and Teddy, though? Don't tell me it's nothing. I have eyes."

I laugh at that. "Was it the log splitting that gave it away?"

"I cannot believe he has known a better way to chop wood for like 15 years and has just been letting us do it wrong the whole time."

"He wanted Dad to like him..."

My brother laughs again. "Ah, sis. He wanted to avoid the deep, uncomfortable silence that comes along with contradicting Rob Evers."

Is that how Teddy sees my dad? Is that how Chris sees him? "I don't know about that, Chris. It's like anything else. I thought the chopping was more about you all bonding out there or whatever."

"Yeah, well, now we can bond with fewer splinters and torn muscles." He groans.

"Oh, you never tore a muscle, you big baby."

"I came pretty close! Den had to massage me with their elbows to get the deep knots."

"Hey, now. Hang on while I jot that down to use in my books."

"Perv."

"Love you."

"I love you, too. But seriously. What's up with you and Ted? You guys okay?"

I sigh and settle deeper into the cot, hoping Chris doesn't recognize the sound of the canvas squeaking. "We will be. We're working on it."

"Okay. Well I'm glad. Let me know if you need anything."

"I needed a good conversation tonight."

"I aim to please!"

When we hang up, I feel more unsettled than before I called.

25

TEDDY

I stare at the email on my monitor, stunned into inaction. My admin wants me to reschedule marriage counseling to meet with a big client last-minute.

A month ago, this would have been a foregone conclusion. Obviously work would have come first. But a month ago, my wife was still living at my house and I wasn't fully aware that my personal life was in injury time.

I think about the sacrifices I made to get here—Vice President of the company. This should give me fulfillment. This should be the thing I've been working toward since I vowed to never again work manual labor. But all it got me was misery.

I don't want to miss my session with Pam. I want to unpack what happened at Thanksgiving. I want to figure out why I can't even rail my wife when she's begging for it.

I write back to José. *Sorry. This appointment is important. Can Yvonne cover the meeting?*

An agonizing minute passes, and my mind creates doom scenarios like me immediately getting fired or blackballed by the client...but another email comes in from José: *Gotcha. Yvonne said she can cover. No sweat.*

No sweat.

I prioritized my marriage and my career didn't crumble.

The fact that this feels like such a big deal seems like something I should definitely bring up with Pam.

So I grab my pea coat and head to Shadyside, navigating the mid-day traffic and managing to avoid a backup from a collapsed bridge. I park out front just as Chloe rounds the corner on foot, her nose pink from the chill, sticking out above her fluffy scarf.

"You look adorable, like an elf." I grin, poking her white puffy coat and then noticing she's wearing leggings. Her ass always looks amazing in leggings.

Chloe smiles. "I just took a class with Piper. I hope I don't stink."

I open the door to Pam's house and hold it for her. "I'm sure you smell great." We walk back into the office together and I hang my coat on the hook. Chloe keeps hers on, saying she needs a few more minutes to get warm. I feel my own rush of heat when she sits next to me again. We're making progress there.

"How was your holiday?" Pam cuts right to the chase and Chloe opens her mouth to say something, but I raise my hand like we're in math class or something. Pam nods to me.

"I wanted to share something that happened today." I tell them about honoring the appointment, not canceling. I guess I was expecting more excitement from Chloe about this, but she frowns.

"Chloe, what do you think about Teddy keeping his commitment to our work?" Pam leans forward on her stool, her clipboard balanced between her knees and her elbows.

"It pisses me off that they would ask him to move his

appointment to accommodate someone who decided to breeze through last minute." Chloe rips off her scarf and flings it over the back of the couch. "I feel like business people are always doing that, assuming the current changes direction to flow their way."

"Hmm." Pam nods. "That's a strong statement from you. Would you like to elaborate?"

She turns to face me on the couch. "I talked to my brother last night. He said something about how I'm never assertive. He made me feel like I let people walk all over me."

"Chris said that?" I feel protective of her, even as I can see some truth in his words. Chloe rarely makes a fuss.

"He was talking about Dad and how...I don't know. He made it sound like I always do what other people say." She turns back to face Pam. "I really think I'm pretty easygoing. I don't have strong opinions about stuff and people in my life really seem to, so I don't see what's wrong with going with the flow."

"Another water reference." Pam jots something down on her clipboard. "I'm wondering how this pride in being easygoing relates to the anger you felt when Teddy pushed the house in the suburbs?"

Chloe's mouth drops open. I draw in a sharp breath. Have I been taking advantage of Chloe? Am I just another brute force in her life?

We're all quiet for a moment and Pam asks us again how things went at Thanksgiving. "I bucked tradition," I blurt. "I was angry about something Chloe and I discussed and I just didn't feel like doing things the same way we always do." I shrug. "It caused some ripples. There's more water metaphors for you."

"Mmm a stormy sea!" Pam seems delighted.

Chloe explains that her father is a creature of habit. "And you are, too, Bear. You like knowing what's going to happen, where we're going to stop for gas. All of that." She clacks her teeth together. "Oh, god, you're like my dad." She pulls her braid over one shoulder and starts twirling it around her hand. "I guess I do sort of go along with what Dad says, and with what Teddy says. What's the point in causing a fuss?"

Pam smiles and leans forward. "You tell me, Chloe. What's the point?"

Chloe looks back and forth between me and Pam as I think about the reality of her words. Her father is assertive and picky and...I am, too.

Pam prods again. "What happened when Ted bucked tradition, as you say?" When nobody says anything, Pam prods, "Was anyone angry?"

Chloe frowns. "My dad was confused. But it seemed fine."

"Mmm." Pam studies her notebook. "And then today, when Ted set a boundary at work, nobody was angry?"

I shrug. "Not that they expressed to me."

Pam nods her head and smiles. "Is it fair to say that sometimes, standing up for our wants and needs allows others in our lives to practice their own adaptability?"

Chloe looks like someone punched her. She squeezes her hands into fists, processing all of this as I think about all the things she just went along with, all the times she didn't tell me what she was feeling. "This is bigger than just the house." I whisper the words, but Chloe hears, and turns to look at me, nodding.

Obviously I always feel like there's a justification for my actions. I have a long-term plan, and the career and house and school district are all part of that. Long-term strategy is a huge part of the MBA curriculum—this way of thinking is ground into my bones. But I guess I never stopped running toward the goal long enough to see if Chloe was with me on the field.

Chloe starts to cry and reaches for the box of tissues. "I really like living in the city. And I really like working for myself. I never really felt passionate about, well, anything before. I was just...having a good time."

"You're fun, Chloe. You are a good time. You were fun at work when we worked together."

I'm trying to reassure her, but I don't think that's how she interprets this statement. She shakes her head. "I hated that job." She takes a deep, shuddering breath. "Oh, I've never said that before. But it's true! I was always playing games to keep my mind off the clock. Like, could I type in a group of email addresses faster than the mail merge...lord. It all felt like busywork to me." She squeezes my leg and I stare down at her hand. "I was relieved when I got laid off."

I swallow and place my hand on top of hers. "I didn't realize that." When I tried to reframe everything, tried to tell her it was good timing for us to try getting pregnant, I was really just trying to cheer her up, because I assumed she felt like I did: terrified.

Honestly, I was rattled when Chloe lost her job. All I could focus on was the loss of income, the impact that would have on our retirement savings and all the other things I now see as me scrambling to meet my pyramid of needs, or whatever Pam called it.

"Tell Pam about the house histories." I squeeze Chloe's hand and scoot closer to her on the couch. "I've always thought that was really interesting."

"You did?" She blinks away tears and dabs at her nose with a tissue.

"Well, sure." I turn to Pam. "Soon after she got laid off, Chloe started researching old buildings in Pittsburgh, but also the people who lived there and the stories behind them. All sorts of interesting stuff like teen runaways and ads for governesses and people falling off scaffolding to their death."

Chloe smiles. "I started with our neighbors. The Stag family was really curious about who owned their house when it was built, and one day I realized I could probably help them figure that out. I had the time..." Chloe looks at me and I smile. Chloe tells Pam how she found newspaper clippings about the family who built the house—another brood of rowdy boys like the Stag brothers always in the paper for shenanigans involving livestock and refuse.

"That was the first one. I loved researching it and they loved having it. Tim and Alice Stag really spread the word." She shrugs. "It was good having something part-time when we were trying to get pregnant. People paid me to research their property, their business locations."

Pam nods and makes notes. "But that's not what you're doing for work now?"

Chloe bites her lip. "It sort of morphed. The stories I was finding were all so layered. I started wondering about the side stories, the things that weren't written down in the old wills and court records." She shrugs. "I started making up whatever details weren't on paper and eventually I had a book."

"She's got three books," I brag, surprising myself by the amount of pride I actually feel at my wife's body of work so far.

Chloe nods. "Yeah. I'm writing a series set in Pittsburgh in the late 18th century." She winces. "It's going really well, but I'm not being a good financial steward."

I laugh at her phrasing. "You sound like you've been hanging out with Logan." Pam looks confused, so I explain, "Chloe's friend is CFO at a tech company."

Pam leans back on her stool and crosses one ankle over her knee. I see that she's wearing wool elf booties and resist the urge to nudge Chloe and point. "I think you've both done a lot of mental work today." Pam nods. "I'd like to continue this next week, really keep this momentum going."

ON THE SIDEWALK OUTSIDE, I lean against my SUV, rubbing my hands together in the cold as I look at my wife, remembering she walked here. "You want a ride home?" Chloe kicks some gravel around with her sneaker and shakes her head. I hold my arms out for a hug, my face a question until Chloe steps into my arms. I hold her tightly and we just stand there like that for a few beats. "That was really heavy in there."

"I'm glad you told José to fuck off." Chloe's voice is muffled where she has her face pressed into my shoulder.

I laugh. "I was a little more diplomatic than that, Chlo."

She steps back and sighs. "I know you were."

I take a deep breath. "I didn't see before, how pushy I was being about everything. I took it for granted that you were running the same plays as me and I didn't stop to notice that you changed your strategy."

She rolls her eyes. "We can stop with the soccer metaphors, Bear."

"Okay, well, I want you to know I've been thinking a lot about all the stuff with my parents, about how it was for me, growing up, and how that informs my behavior now, or whatever." I smile, hoping she'll appreciate me using some of Pam's language.

Chloe leans against the car beside me, a smile teasing her own lips. "What comes next?"

I shrug. "You tell me. I'll put the house up for sale. Or not. But my path is back to you, Chloe. That's my priority."

"What about your balls?"

I blow out a breath. "Well, frankly, I've been putting off thinking about those."

She shakes her head. "We can't go back to avoiding that."

I nod. "What if we table it until we figure out the house? Like...where I will live if I sell it?" I arch a brow, hopeful that she'll insist I move back in with her immediately.

She frowns. "How about you list the house and we'll work through a fertility discussion before closing."

I laugh and kiss her on the forehead before I can think twice about it. "You'd be a shark in a contract negotiation, babe."

"Nah."

"You have a preference for a realtor?" It feels like a good idea to ask her since she wasn't even part of the conversation the last time around.

Chloe nods. "What about Sara, who helped us buy the Highland Park house?"

"She was nice. I'll give her a call."

"You want to come check on the mushrooms?" Chloe smiles and I nod. We walk together and spray down our shiitake project before I head back to the office. I don't want to get my hopes up, but it seems like we can get a second life out of this kit if we keep up the hard work.

26

TEDDY

Co-Ed Rec Soccer!

Someone left the neon green flyer on the counter in the kitchen at work. I might never have noticed it if I'd been there for lunch, among the busy rush of my colleagues clambering for our corporate chef's daily hot feast.

But now, as I warm my leftovers up in the microwave, the flyer seems targeted just for me. Co-ed. Usually this means one or two token women to meet a quota, but Chloe could always hang. I think about how much fun we had coaxing a log of mushrooms to life, how much more intense it could be to work with her on the field.

I need to make amends with Chloe, for the dog, for all of it. For bulldozing through plans and not including her until late in the game. This soccer event feels like it has potential as a peace offering.

I call her, but it goes straight to voicemail. Shit. She's either writing or deep in the county archives with no reception. I bite my lip, not wanting to steamroll her with another forced choice but not wanting to miss our chance at a spot in the game, either.

I decide to sign us both up for the game, vowing to cancel if Chloe seems the least bit uninterested. An 8pm start time on a field in the city will be tough for me on a Thursday, especially with a long drive home at the end of it. But I think it'll be worthwhile. I close my eyes and remember watching Chloe run around with the women's alumni a few weeks ago, the joy on her face as she kicked a corner to her friend Lucy, who tapped it into the goal.

I text a picture of the flyer to my wife.

> Want to check this out?

Her response is immediate, startling me since I just called her with no luck.

CHLOE PRESTON:

> Oh my god where did you find that? Yes! Definitely yes! Should I buy you new shin guards? Or, I guess should I buy me new ones...

I grin, feeling like a kid about to attend a professional sporting event.

> Nah, you keep the guards. I'll make the moves.

CHLOE PRESTON:

> We better be on separate teams so I can smoke you, Preston!

> Count on it, Preston.

> Actually, no. I really want to be on your team, babe.

CHLOE PRESTON:

Okay, okay.

She sends a series of excited face emojis and I make plans to meet her at our city house after work tomorrow to eat and change before the game. She even agrees to let the dog hang out in his crate while we play soccer, especially after I share painstaking details about his house-training progress.

"Is it weird that I feel nervous?" Chloe bounces in the seat beside me, already wearing cleats and looking adorable in a beanie, puffy coat and leggings. Of course she'd wear the distractingly tight leggings. I send up a silent prayer again that I get to be on the same team as her so there's less chance I'm caught off guard staring at her ass.

"I believe that feeling you're experiencing is excitement." I reach for our bag with our water bottles and hand warmers. I marvel at all the small touches Chloe put in to our night out together, from scrounging up packets to warm our hands and toes to matching PRESTON t-shirts we can wear over our warm layers.

I park near the sports complex in Schenley Park and we walk up the hill together toward the turf field. The atmosphere is so familiar I almost want to cry. How could I let go of this for so long? All around me, people are stretching and warming up with balls, kicking passes to each other or jogging back and forth across the field working on footwork skills.

"Hey, you guys new?" A woman with braided pigtails approaches, grinning. "I'm Cyndie. Are you the Prestons?"

"That's us." I drape an arm around Chloe's shoulder and

she snuggles up close to me. I can tell she's feeling the same sort of overwhelm and familiarity. We should have found an adult league to join ages ago. Somewhere in between grad school and asserting my fucked-up life plan on our marriage, I lost the stuff that makes us click: healthy competition.

Cyndie assigns us to the red team and hands us a pair of mesh pinneys. Chloe frowns at our custom t-shirts, but I nudge her with my shoulder. "We can wear them to counseling." I shrug. "Or Thanksgiving. Your dad would love that."

She laughs and I help her into the pinney, glad I could ease her disappointment and still let her know I saw her effort in making the shirts.

And then we take the field together. We start out in the mid-field, side by side. I can't keep anyone's name straight on my team, but it hardly matters once Chloe has the ball. The group is pretty evenly matched, skill-wise, apart from Chloe. I lose myself watching her beat out defenders, making moves and practically dancing up the sideline until she's in range to pass to our striker.

I trap a high ball with my chest and slide it to my wife without looking, sensing her there beside me before I dart ahead to get another pass back from her up the side. Like she read my mind, she sends the ball exactly where I'm headed. I take two steps, plant, and strike the ball toward the tiny goal this group uses for their pickup matches. It soars through the torn park net, right out the back and into the bleachers.

"Ha!" I pump a fist in the air. "Babe, awesome pass!" I turn to look for her, but she's on me, throwing her arms around my waist and squealing with delight. Chloe is ecstatic, and it's contagious.

The game lasts for another hour until people start to

collapse from exhaustion. On the sideline, I laugh as Chloe's head steams in the chilly night air. My breath comes out in a white puff as I wait my turn for our shared water bottle.

I chug gratefully when Chloe hands me the bottle, watching her chest rise and fall as her heart rate slows after the match. Around us, the players give a chorus of "good game" and "see you next time" but I only focus on Chloe. Chloe, who comes alive on the field where there is only one objective and one thing to worry about: go forward.

"I have to tell you something." I lean closer to her, resting my forehead against her steaming hair. "I signed us up to play tonight before I heard back from you. But I was fully prepared to cancel if you weren't interested."

"Teddy." She puts both hands on my thighs, which clench beneath her touch. "This is an amazing surprise."

I swallow thickly. "I don't know if I can tell the difference."

She shrugs. "So don't surprise me. Always ask first." She climbs to her feet and reaches for my hand. We walk to the car with our arms around each other, smelling like sweat and deodorant and musty pinney.

"I loved that give-and-go we had early on in the match," she says, turning her body to face mine in the car.

"Oh you mean when I scored so hard I tore the net?"

She laughs. "No. What I loved was that we were so in sync. You knew I was going to pass it up the line. I knew you were going to run up the line."

I nod as I turn out of the park toward home. Toward her home. Our home? Maybe someday. "It felt pretty damn good."

I follow Chloe to the door and lean on the porch rail as she unlocks the house. I run my hand along the wood she recently repainted. I admit that this would be a great porch for a family. We bought our first house on a quiet street with a ton of kids running around. I sigh and shake my head, not wanting to go there. Not tonight.

The door clicks as Chloe pushes it open a bit. "Thank you again for this, Teddy. Tonight was amazing."

She hesitates, a shy expression on her face. I feel a little bit like I did the first night I took her out. I remember then how she told me I had better kiss her already, so I edge closer to her at the door. I reach to cup her cheek, my palm warm against her cold skin. She smiles, her eyes twinkling in the porch light.

I lean in, pressing my lips to hers, tasting sweat and Gatorade on her lips. I moan softly and deepen the kiss, my tongue swiping gently inside her mouth. Chloe makes a high-pitched, satisfied sound I can feel rumbling up and down my spine. I pull back and kiss her hand before things get out of control. I want to end tonight on a high note.

Once I stop kissing my wife, I can hear the excited clicks and yips from the dog in the house. "Hey, pal, I see you there." I walk into the entryway and stoop to open the crate. I scoop him into my arms and turn to see Chloe holding his leash. I smile and gather everything up to take him back with me.

By the time she waves and shuts the door, I feel hopeful that things might eventually be okay.

27

TEDDY

I NEED HELP. Lots of it. I keep doing the same shit again and again and digging myself into deeper holes with Chloe and what I need is a plan to keep us on track.

Only, my plans usually lead to me barreling head first into something that excludes Chloe. I don't know how to break this cycle.

It's Saturday morning and I've got nothing to do because I'm selling my house and my wife lives somewhere else. I roll over in bed and find the dog wagging his tail.

"How'd you get out of the crate?"

He licks my hand, startling me as he jumps up onto Chloe's pillow.

I drag my hands through my hair and growl, and then laugh when the dog mimics my sounds.

I have absolutely no idea what to do now. I've clearly reached a point where whatever I think is the right idea, I should do the opposite of that.

That soccer game felt like a turning point. I know we can click together again. I felt it. I remember that I do actually have to be out of the house by eleven because the realtor is doing an open house.

Within hours of texting Sara, she had a whole package put together for what we could expect selling the suburban house. I was a little shell shocked by how much more money she thought we could get than when I bought it a few years ago. Apparently a lot of corporate folks have the same life-plan as me. She thinks we'll get offers this weekend. If I ever get out of here.

I hop out of bed and quickly straighten the covers. I glance around the room. The whole house is practically sterile. I'm barely here, and the housekeeper was just in the other day. I don't think there's anything I need to do before families start combing through my closets.

I wonder if I should call Chloe, see if she wants to hang out with me this morning. I hate that I feel so much hesitation about spending time with my own wife.

The dog licks my ankles as I fill his bowl in the kitchen. I ruffle his ears and watch him eat, wishing I knew who to call about all this stuff.

Chloe's always saying her friends help her sort through big ideas. What do they call themselves? Floof? "Foof." I say it out loud and the dog yips, his bark sounding a lot like the word for Chloe's friend group. "Foof," I repeat. "Foof."

Maybe that's what I need—advice from people my wife already trusts to have her back. I look at the dog again. "Are you allowed inside a bar?" He licks my hand in response and I nod.

I drive toward Bridges and Bitters prepared to beg Esther and crew to meet me outside if I can't bring the dog in for some pooch-hooch.

·   ·   ·

I WAVE at Esther through the window, the dog in my arms. She raises a dark brow at me and so I pick up the dog's paw, making him wave, too. She beckons me inside, still looking confused. "What's up, Theodore?" She leans against a table, arms crossed, a white towel dangling from her jeans pocket. It's early in the day and nobody has wandered into the bar yet. "Who's your furry friend?"

I approach Esther, who skritches the dog's fur between his ears, earning a few licks. "He doesn't have a name yet. I... bought him for Chloe. As a gesture."

Esther sucks air in through her teeth, making a cringe face. "That seems impulsive."

"Yeah." I continue petting the dog. "Hey, can I get a drink?"

She scowls as she considers, and then tips her head toward the bar. "Pull up a seat. I'm going to call for reinforcements."

I set the dog on the stool beside me and he mimics my posture, putting his tiny paws on the edge of the bar. Esther laughs. I consider asking her if she wants a guard dog. She emerges from the back with a bowl of nuts and a jug of something.

"This is a friend's beer. I figure you can help me taste-test it while we wait for Piper and Sam and whoever else is nearby."

My cheeks flush. "Oh. I don't know about all that."

Esther raps her knuckles on the bar. "If you came here looking for me, things are pretty bad. Am I wrong?" I frown at my lap. "Hey." She snaps her fingers. "Better out than in."

As she says this, the front door opens and Piper bursts in, clad in workout gear and looking sweaty. Esther laughs. "Isn't it like 20 degrees outside? Where's your coat?"

"You caught me after kettlebells," Piper says, sinking into

the stool on the other side of the dog, and then noticing him. "Oh my lord in heaven, who is this?" The dog immediately starts licking her sweaty hands and face as Piper coos and praises him for being a good boy. Esther pours three pints from the growler and raises hers for a toast.

Piper and I clink glasses with her and take a sip of the beer, which is hoppy and fruity and goes down smooth. I smack my lips. "That's nice." Esther nods approvingly and then crosses her arms, waiting.

"So," I stutter. "I'm sure you both know Chloe moved out." They nod. "I used to think this was only about the baby stuff. I'm guessing she told you that, too." More nods and a few sips of beer to fill the silence. I drop a hand to the dog's fur, finding comfort in the warm curls beneath my fingers. "I think mostly I have a lot of baggage about growing up poor."

Esther shrugs. "That tracks. Hunger sucks and all that." She gestures for me to continue.

"I've been operating in starvation mode for a long time, even though I haven't been hungry in a decade." I think they both know I was never truly hungry for anything except—apparently—comfort. But that's not true, is it? I was starving for success, for belonging. I was hungry for a different life. "Somewhere along the line, Chloe slipped from being my partner on an adventure into someone I felt like I had to protect at all costs. And, well, I'm paying the costs now."

I set the beer on the bar and am surprised when Piper puts a reassuring hand on my shoulder and squeezes. "I just keep hoarding symbols of wealth. That's what our marriage counselor calls it. The house and the graduate degree and all that."

"Nothing wrong with wanting to get ahead in life." Esther takes another sip of her own beer, studies it, and then pulls a notepad out of her back pocket to jot something down. Then she looks up at me. "I'm going to be honest, Ted. I don't think you're in the life you want to get ahead of."

"Yes, that's all becoming clear. My question for you is what do I do about it? What do I actually do to get back on track? With Chloe?"

Piper spins her glass around on the bar and then gasps when Esther quickly lifts the cup and slides a napkin beneath it. Piper looks at me. "You two focused on *you* for a long while. Grad school, the promotion...the move." I wince, embarrassed now at my behavior in dragging us into a new house without discussing it first. I was just so certain Chloe wanted the same sort of family life I did. Not sure how I became certain of that. What did Pam say? I've had my blinders on so I could sow the field in a straight line or whatever?

Piper continues. "I think it could be supportive of you to focus on *her* for a little. I know she'd never say so, but it hurt her feelings when you didn't come to her launch party last time."

Samantha had texted me a few times about an event at the history museum to celebrate Chloe's book. "I remember hearing about a party...I just didn't understand why it was so important I guess." It also didn't seem possible in the final days leading up to my promotion, and Sam definitely had the event planning well in hand. She always plans things for the gals. I sigh. "I wish the timing of that could have been different."

Esther nods. "If Sam had sent you date options, would you really have made the time to go?"

I hold up my palms. "Mea culpa. So what do I do? Throw her a book party for the next one?"

Piper snorts. "She's going to have people throwing her galas for her by then. Have you seen her sales rank?"

"I'm not really sure how book sales ranks are tabulated..."

Piper shrugs. "Sometimes Chloe brings numbers to Foof meetings. She's got a *lot* of pre-orders."

Esther nods. "Best-seller list pre-orders."

"Hm." I pull the dog all the way into my lap and ruffle his ears as he licks my jeans, the weirdo. "When you say Chloe will have people...is she planning to hire staff?" Esther and Piper gesture that they don't know, but an idea starts to form. "Hmm. This is enlightening. Hey, can one of you give me Logan's contact info? I want to ask her for a referral."

Esther grins and pulls out her notepad again to write down the number, but Piper teases her about being a luddite and holds up her phone. "Unlock your phone, Tedster. I'll air drop you her number."

28

CHLOE

I HEAR Teddy's individual ring-tone and realize I forgot to silence my phone here in the archives. "Hello?" I whisper into the mic trying not to disturb anyone around me. Then I remember that the people around me are the ones who shove past me in the security line and treat me like crap. "Ted?" I say it louder this time, feeling assertive.

"Yes, is this Chloe Petals the independent publisher?"

I frown and look at the phone to make sure it's my husband calling. It is. I recognize his voice. Why is he being weird? "What's going on?"

"Well, this is Theodore Preston, MBA, calling to see if your business would be interested in a consultation. Free of charge, of course."

"Consultation? Teddy, what are you doing?" I slip back to whispering and look over my shoulders to make sure nobody is in my vicinity. Then I notice the time and realize most of the other folks have left by now. I've only got a few hours left before they close. Damn. I still haven't found the information I need about soldiers' pay in this region in the early 1800s.

Ted clears his throat. "Ms. Petals, did you know many entrepreneurs lack formal training in business administration? Small business owners like yourself have creativity and drive for days, but perhaps have a skill gap when it comes to financials or forecasting..."

He drifts off like he's waiting for me to say something. "I'm so confused, Bear."

Teddy laughs. "I am offering to talk about your business with you. See if I can support you in any way, or just listen and be excited with you about your year ahead."

I bite my lip. I'm worried about what his form of support might look like. Scandal Sheet Press is mine and I want to be in charge of everything about it. Including, I guess, its potential tax penalties. I groan. "You won't get bossy?"

"You can't see right now, but I'm giving the Scout sign to swear on my honor that I will not get bossy. Where you at, babe?"

I hear footsteps echoing along the gross tile floor and I look over my shoulder. I drop the phone when I see Teddy in the room, his head glowing in a cloud of dust near the flickering fluorescent lights. "How did you find me?"

He shrugs. "You weren't home, and I remembered dropping you off by Mr. Rogers. I asked the security guard if she knew you."Any concerns I might have about my husband's sleuthing skills are erased by my excitement to see him in the middle of a work day. I can't help the smile that melts over my face. "Can I sit?"

I nod, hanging up my phone and tucking it back in my bag. Teddy reaches across the table and squeezes my hand. He pulls a small notebook from his suit pocket and clicks open a pen. The whole image is very sexy, him in his sharp suit preparing to take notes. "I wanted to let you know I talked to Logan," he says, sliding me a business card. "She recommended a tax pro who specializes in small businesses. This would be someone you hire for Chloe Petals, separate from Chloe Preston."

I stare down at the card, a feeling of relief washing over me. I was so worried about giving my financials to Teddy, about having him pore over my expenses and ad spend the way he does our charitable giving. I don't even have an explanation for why I'd keep my business so fiercely secret. "Should I call her now?" I feel tears well in my eyes as I look up at him.

Ted shakes his head. "Maybe we can talk a bit first?" I nod. "I don't know if you knew that I did consults with small businesses in grad school. It was part of our graduation requirements."

"I guess I never asked you about the particulars." I swallow and fiddle with my braid. He tells me about a typical consult, how the business owner would lay out the basics like their corporate structure and some short- and long-term goals.

"Would you be interested in talking through any of that, Chloe? I would love to recommend someone if you didn't want it to be me..."

"I could tell you," I whisper. Then I clear my throat and say it louder. "My publishing company is called Scandal Sheet Press."

He grins. "That's funny. Very clever."

I nod. "My goal this year is to publish my third book, also in audio, and maybe start some foreign translations for the series." I remember the agent email. "I also turned down a fancy-pants agent who wanted to woo me and buy my book rights."

Teddy arches a brow. "Buy your rights?"

I shake my head rapidly. "I'm not ready to give up creative control."

He smiles. "I like your creative work." Teddy asks me questions about my business structure and seems impressed that I set up the LLC paperwork by myself. He doesn't mention the fact that I haven't kept up with the sole proprietor taxes on my royalties.

"Your tax pro should help you set up a system to pay yourself a salary," Teddy explains. "You can choose what to reinvest and what to pay yourself, and how often."

Eventually he asks me what I'm working on today and I show him some of the wills I was reading along with property transfers. "I'm trying to figure out what sort of house and property a soldier might have had, so I can weave that into the plot of the book."

Teddy adjusts his tie. "You mean so you know what kind of breeches Linus could afford to buy."

I flush and nod. "Yep."

He arches a brow. "And maybe whether he could buy Sally silk stockings?"

I swat at his arm and shiver, wiggling in my seat. I hadn't realized he'd been reading my book, but I like that he has, that he knows my characters and what they've been up to, in and out of their breeches.

Teddy swallows and places his palms on the table. "I wanted to run another idea past you." I nod and he takes a deep breath. "It really seems like you need some dedicated space for Scandal Sheet Press. Our house in Highland Park is so small, with just the two big bedrooms and that third one is basically a closet."

I frown, considering. I didn't have a home office when we lived there. I had just begun my house history work and did most of my writing and research from the couch. I only really got an office when we moved into the McMansion. "It was nice having an office," I concede.

He nods. "Maybe we can ask Sara to show us some houses in the city? With more rooms and space for you to have a proper office?"

My heart soars at the thought of this, of us looking together for the perfect home, one that's in the city with space and no huge commute for him. I gasp. "I love that idea." I fly up and out of my seat, the legs screeching along the floor, and rush around the table to grip Teddy's coat. "I love that idea so much."

He surprises me again when he tugs me into his lap, right there in the public archives. "I'm glad," he whispers against my ear.

I inhale sharply when I feel the ridge of his arousal in his pants. I lick my lips, glancing around the empty room again. I close my eyes and listen, but I don't even hear the squeaky wheels of the carts for other researchers or staff returning books to the shelves. I think we are alone.

29

TEDDY

I CERTAINLY DIDN'T COME DOWN HERE with the intention of seducing Chloe where she's working. I mostly wanted to drop off the business card and see what she thought about us finding another house together.

But when she rushed around the table all flushed and excited, my body responded.

I squeeze her hips as I pull her down tighter against my lap. She keeps looking around like she's checking for intruders. It seemed pretty deserted when I came in. That's how I found her so easily. Her voice carried through the room, empty except for her beloved record books.

When Chloe turns her head to the right, I lean in and nip at her neck. She coos and I lick the red mark I made with my teeth. "Want to know something?" Chloe's eyebrows shoot up and she nods. "I've always wanted to make out with the CEO of a corporation at her work."

Chloe's laugh soars out of her, filling the room as she seems to melt against my chest. "I didn't know that about you." She makes to stand up but I hold her still and kiss her.

I like the feel of her hands on my shoulders, her fingertips on my neck and in my hair.

She wriggles around, writhing in those damn leggings and when I look down, I can see her nipples hard inside her t-shirt. "Shit, Chloe." I'm so hard it's painful, and it's become increasingly obvious that we are in public. Why did I pull her into my lap like this?

I groan and drop my head back, but Chloe hops out of my lap and tugs on my tie. "Come on," she says, nodding her head toward one of the aisles.

I gingerly stand up and I'm practically limping as my dick presses against the zipper in my pants. "Hang on," I croak, breathing heavily as I try to follow her.

Chloe pushes one hand on the door of a supply closet and my jaw drops as she looks over her shoulder. "Poor Teddy," she says. "Does it hurt?" I nod, short movements of my head as she tugs my hand and pulls me into the closet. It's surprisingly spacious and blessedly empty. Chloe clicks the door shut and doesn't turn on the light. The frosted glass window lets in enough light that I can see a wicked gleam in her eye. "Do you want me to kiss it?"

She sinks to her knees on the tile floor, a vision of chestnut hair and peachy skin on the green linoleum. Chloe yanks down my zipper and flicks open my belt and then my erection is in her palm, twitching. "Christ, fucking hell. Oh god," I moan when her mouth slides over my tip. I feel her tongue flatten and trace the head of my cock and it's been so long. So long.

"Mmm," Chloe mumbles as she licks and sucks, bobbing her perfect head up and down while her palms press against my thighs. My breath comes in tiny bursts.

"Chloe." My voice is strangled. "Babe, it's too much. I'm going to—"

She pops off the end of my cock and looks up at me, her big, brown eyes brimming with lust. "It's okay, Bear. I want you to come."

She dives back in and I stuff one hand in my mouth to smother my moans. I drop a gentle hand to my wife's head and a few pumps of that velvety heat later, I feel the orgasm explode from the base of my spine. I erupt into Chloe's mouth, abs clenching, thighs shaking as she swallows every drop.

Chloe sinks back onto her heels and giggles. She claps her hands. "I've always wanted to do that here. In the archives, I mean."

Any scrap of dignity I had crumbles away and I sink to the floor beside her, my pants undone and drooping. I yelp when my bare ass hits the floor. Chloe giggles again. "It's just so hot that you came here to find me and plan things with me, Bear."

I can't move. I can barely see. I just had my first Chloe-induced orgasm in months and the entire thing overwhelms me so entirely I worry I might pass out. I lean my head against the wall of the closet. "I'm sorry I didn't do this sooner," I say, eventually.

I crack open one eye and see that Chloe has shifted to sit beside me. She rests her head on my shoulder and sighs, then she looks down at my undignified lap and laughs.

"You think this is funny?" I stick a thumb in the waist of her leggings and snap them. She squeals and tries to squirm away from me. "Let's see your pantalettes."

30

CHLOE

I PRACTICALLY PURR as Teddy tugs my leggings down my hips. I feel so naughty, lying down on the dusty floor of the supply closet in the building where I conduct my research. Of course, the leggings snag and stick to my thighs, but Teddy is undeterred.

I lie on my back and stroke his hair as he works diligently, methodically to scoot them down my legs. He notices my lack of underwear and sits up, his mouth dropping open in an oh.

"Chloe Preston! You're not even wearing pantalettes!" He drops a hand as if to cover me but quickly changes course and begins to stroke and pet all the places I've missed his touch.

"They bunch up in my leggings," I huff out. "Oh, shit, that feels good, Bear."

He leans forward again, investigating. I peek up at my husband and notice his body is springing back to life, as if all the parts of him are interested in this new discovery. "Is this all the time? Whenever you're wearing the leggings?"

I don't answer, because I'm drowning in the sensation

he's drawing out of me, but then he stops his hand and gives me a look. I've seen this look before. Teddy Preston makes this face when he's about to bend my body into a pretzel and make me come until I scream.

"They have a cotton crotch," I spit out, my hands fluttering around on the floor, reaching for him.

"That's not an answer, Chloe." Teddy presses one hand into my stomach, inching my shirt up and exposing the skin of my tummy briefly before he bends and kisses it. His mouth is so soft, so gentle. I groan and reach for him, thrusting my hips up, desperate.

"No," I blurt. "No, I never wear anything under the leggings."

"Oh, fucking hell, Chloe." He drops down so he's leaning over me, his dress shirt tails tangling with my t-shirt, both our lower halves naked, our pants bunched around our ankles. It should be ridiculous, but I've never been more turned on.

When Teddy slides a finger inside me, I keen, low moans bursting out of me and Teddy snaps his eyes to mine. "Shhh, babe." His finger stills and I nod, smashing my lips together when he begins to stroke me again.

"I'm so close already." It's true. I've been on edge for months, walking around sexually frustrated. Taking him into my mouth in the closet nudged me that much closer. I can still taste him in my mouth as I try not to scream with his fingers inside me. "Teddy, please!"

My words come out like a plea, a desperate wail, and I hold my breath as he reaches for his cock, circling my slick folds with the tip. He's hard again, as hard as before. He slides the tip inside me and both of us cry out.

"Oh, fuck, Chloe." Teddy hovers above me, arms trembling as he slides home a millimeter at a time.

"Yes," I say. "Yes." I drop my hands to his ass and palm his taut cheeks, trying to push him against me, trying to hurry him along, but he will not be rushed.

"I dream of you, of feeling your perfect pussy," he whispers, sliding in another notch. "This is better than anything I imagined."

"Oh, Teddy, it feels exactly right." My chest is pulsing as my breaths come shallow and quickly. I feel like I'm 85 minutes into a soccer match, adrenaline the only thing driving me forward.

Finally, he's fully seated inside me. He rests his forehead against mine and I tip my head so I can kiss him. I feel his hands on my face, holding me. "Oh, god, Chloe." I tilt my hips and start to move, feeling the firm sting of him filling me, stretching me open.

My movements spur him into action and soon Teddy is pounding me into the floor as I cling to his butt. I want so many things—to hook a leg around his waist or press my heels into the floor and drive up to meet his hips, but both of us are tangled in our pants. All we have is this—thrusting and practically sobbing as we collide.

"I love you, Bear." It's always been true. Love has always been there, even if a lot of other emotions have swirled on top of my affection.

A tear rolls down his face as he jerks his hips. "I love you, too, Chloe. Oh, fuck I love you so much."

Teddy reaches between our bodies, finds the tight pearl of my clit and circles it with the pad of his finger, the motion familiar and thrilling in equal measure. He strums and pats until my body starts to quake. "I can feel you milking my cock." His words come out as grunts now as he thrusts and rubs. "Come for me, Chloe. Come!"

And I do. I feel a burst of nerves shooting pleasure

through my body in waves. I reach up and pull his face to mine, needing to kiss him so I don't scream his name as I come and come and squeeze him until I fear he won't be able to slide out.

But then I feel Teddy tip over the edge with me, thickening inside me and pulsing. I feel the warm heat of him coming inside me, my name on his lips.

WE'RE both breathing heavily as we try to pull ourselves together. It occurs to me that I've left my stuff just sitting out in a public building—my laptop, phone, purse. All of it is sitting with Teddy's suit coat. I look at the two of us, grinning with dusty knees and sex hair. And I laugh.

I laugh until my throat feels hoarse.

I gesture vaguely at my crotch, hesitating before I pull up my leggings. "I need to get to the bathroom," I say, bummed for the first time that there's not even an old roll of industrial paper towels in this closet.

"Here." Teddy loosens his tie and hands it to me. He dangles the tip of it between my legs.

"Babe, no. That's gross. Right?"

He shrugs. "I'll buy another one. Or I'll get it dry cleaned. It's worth it. Trust me." He kisses my cheek and jumps to his feet, tugging up his pants and tucking in his shirt. A few rubs of his hair and he actually looks decent enough to crack the door open and check if anyone's in the hall.

I dab the tie into the mess and try to get my pants pulled up. I try raking my fingers through my hair but it's no use, so I give up and peek out the crack in the door. "I think we're clear."

He grins and the two of us hold hands, gathering up our things and practically frolicking out of the building.

I'm out of breath navigating down the marble stairs, so old they've been worn unevenly by untold numbers of shoes climbing and descending these steps. People accessing these records, wanting to delve into history. Right now, all I can think about is the future.

"I took the bus," I pant to him, shoving open the door to the mezzanine. We pause together, taking in the grandeur of the old building. The marble is ornately carved. The signs are made of brass with bright curlicues decorating each element, each letter.

Teddy snugs his arm around me, pulling me tight against him. "Can I drive you home? Take you to dinner?"

I smile up at him. "You better feed me after all that."

TEDDY'S ESCALADE HAS A TICKET. He parked in a lane that becomes an extra passing lane during rush hour. He tucks the pink paper into his pocket and smiles. "Worth it, seriously." I shake my head and climb inside. Since the parking spot is actually a right-turn lane at the moment, we just wait for the light to change.

I settle into the leather seats, feeling sleepy and satisfied. "I love that you want to support my business but not barge in and change things."

He smiles, keeping his eyes on the road as he slips along toward the river. And then he scowls. "Oh, crap, I got in the lane for the Fort Duquesne Bridge. I wasn't thinking." He starts to mutter and look for a way to change lanes, tries to scoot through four lanes of rush hour traffic to get himself turned around before he crosses the wrong river.

"Hey," I sit up a little straighter. "Let's just go get the dog and some of your stuff." I pat his leg as he drives. "We can try a sleepover and see how that goes."

"Yeah?" His eyes are wide, incredulous. I nod. "Okay. Okay, I'd really like that, Chloe."

"I figured." He putters along, picking up speed as the traffic eases a bit. "Ooh we can take the carpool lane." We both smile as he cuts the wheel.

31

TEDDY

THE DOG and I are snuggled together with Chloe on a nest of random cushions and blankets on the floor of the living room. We got takeout and ate it naked as the fur ball ran up and down the hall where I barricaded him using chairs and kitchen stools.

Eventually we gave up hope of an encore and brought him into the room with us. "This is really nice, babe." I run my fingers through her hair, luxuriating in the sensation as the strands tickle my skin. "I've missed this."

I yelp as the dog's nails press into my stomach. "Oh, hello," Chloe says, trying to scoot him off my chest. "Yes, you can cuddle, too." She ruffs his fur and he digs in between our heads like he's always been there.

"What about Tony?" I look at him, his bright eyes glinting in the low light.

"He's not a Tony. Don't be ridiculous, Theodore." I feel a little jealous of the dog as Chloe begins to pet him gently. I only just got her hands back on me. I want them to stay there. I try to communicate this to the dog, but he's a sucker for attention, too. "Mmm," Chloe sniffs him. "Maybe Fred."

We fall asleep bickering over names, and eventually her arm does drape back across my body, her hand on my heart, which she's always held in her palm anyway.

CHLOE and I have both always been early risers. It's nearly December, though, and we linger in our floor nest until the sun starts to spill through the living room windows.

"Hey, Bear?"

"Mm?" I run my fingers through her hair, inhaling her scent, luxuriating in this closeness between us.

"I don't think I was ready for parenthood before." I feel her stiffen, like she's girding herself for a big response from me.

Only I don't have a big response. "We wouldn't have been open with each other. I mean if it had happened." I drift off, not sure how to talk about a what-if for something that was never possible to begin with.

"I think that's true," she whispers. "I'm learning a lot right now. Like, Teddy?"

"Yeah, babe?"

She leans up on her forearms in a little cobra yoga pose, eyes big and bright as she stares at me. "I really, really like being an author. More than I ever liked a job before."

I smile, happy about her happiness. "I'm glad, Chlo. It seems like you're pretty good at it."

She runs her nails lightly down my stomach, sending shivers and goosebumps all along my body. "I love that you read my book."

"I loved reading it. Not just the naughty bits—the story was really good."

"Yeah?" She smiles. "Which part was good?"

I shrug. "All of it. I never could quite tell if they'd wind up together...the stakes were so high and it would have been so easy for them to just break up and go their separate ways."

"The hard work is what makes the reward so awesome," she whispers.

I nod and start to kiss her, moaning softly at the delicious familiarity of doing that, when the dog wiggles in between us and starts to yip.

Chloe laughs at first, then frowns. "Will the dog pee our bed?"

I rub my eyes and groan, reaching for my shoes. "Not if I let him out back quickly." I tug on a shirt and shuffle to the door, opening it to the brisk morning. Then I remember this yard doesn't have a fence, so I have to go out there with him and make sure he doesn't run away.

My teeth chatter as I stalk him around the yard, where he examines every blade of grass before taking a leak. This is mundane and sort of miserable, and I am so happy right now I hardly know how to contain myself. This doesn't stress me out like a five-year plan. This feels like something I'm doing, together with Chloe. Like life. Just life.

I realize I forgot to bring a bag out with me for the dog's business, but I feel something warm and soft around my shoulders. I turn to see my wife, smiling as she reaches up to wrap me in a blanket. "You forgot your coat."

The gesture sends my heart soaring, reminds me that Chloe and I are well and truly on the mend. I toss the blanket onto her and convince her to keep an eye on the furball as I dash inside for a paper towel. Once we're all back inside and cleaned up, I start looking around for breakfast and realize Chloe has nothing but oatmeal packets.

I frown at the empty cupboard, but then I remember

where we are: a walkable neighborhood with several options for pastries and fancy coffee. "Should we head over to grab a muffin?"

"Mmm, yes, please." Chloe flings open the closet where we stashed our coats and bags last night. "And what about you? Is your name Muffin?" The dog is clacking circles around Chloe, yipping and wagging his fuzzy tail.

I hook up his leash and open the door, and Chloe follows with the keys. "What about Mocha? He's almost the right color..."

She shakes her head as we begin to walk toward Bryant Street. "I don't really think he should have a food name." A few neighbors pause to greet the dog, squatting to tickle his chin or scritch that spot between his ears.

The dog tugs on the leash to head up a side street we don't usually take, but I'm not in a hurry so I follow his lead. Chloe wanders behind me, muttering potential names. "Oswald? Strider? Wiggles?"

We both stop in front of a house with a FOR SALE sign out front and the nameless pooch puts his paws up on the fence and yips. "Huh." I lean on the fence beside him. The house is large, with two full stories and what looks like a third-floor bedroom.

"It's got a driveway," Chloe coos. "In the city! A driveway!" I nod at the flat expanse of concrete. Off-street parking in this neighborhood is hard to come by. "Teddy, imagine not having to shovel out a parking spot that someone steals as soon as we leave for work?"

I drape an arm around Chloe's shoulders and point to the building behind the driveway. "How about that little cottage, though?" The house has a separate building connected by a pergola to the main house. There's a patio between the buildings, hung with fairy lights.

"This is so charming!" Chloe claps her hands and stretches on her tip-toes to look around. "Could that be an office?"

"It could be whatever you want it to be, love." I scratch my chin as the dog wags his tail and tries to wriggle between the black iron bars of the fence. "This would be a good yard for a dog."

Chloe swallows and smiles, her eyes a little watery. "Or a kid," she says.

I feel my heart surge, not with shame or panic, but with hope. "Or a kid," I repeat. "Someday."

CHLOE RUNS AHEAD to the bakery to grab breakfast while I stand in front of the house and text our realtor the address and ask if we can get a showing. We head back to our house and settle in at the counter, chewing and sipping in silence as we stare at my phone, waiting to see what Sara says.

I pat Chloe's leg. "Tell me more about your thoughts on that house. I want to make sure I'm not bulldozing."

She grins. "Not bulldozing. You're right that we need more space, no matter what shape our family takes. And that guest house!"

"You mean detached office space." I grin, enjoying the satisfied expression that transforms her face. I clear my throat, thinking over the last time I sat waiting to hear back from a realtor about buying a house. "I didn't grow up in a family where anyone asked anyone else for input."

She nods. "I know that."

"I don't think you did, either, though. Maybe the decisions weren't as high-stakes, but..." I shrug. "I got used to just acting, snapping." She takes a sip of her coffee and nods. "I'm working on it, is what I'm saying. I'd like to keep working on it."

"I appreciate that, Bear." Chloe takes a deep breath. "I want to work on speaking up sooner, too. We both need to communicate about—well, about everything."

I raise my coffee cup to her in a toast. "To slowing down."

She grins. "To speaking up."

We clink glasses and sip, looking each other in the eye for luck. I smile, remembering that she taught me this toasting tradition back in college. "I keep thinking of more soccer metaphors."

"Let's hear 'em." She rests her chin on her hand, elbow on the counter as she smiles at me.

"You have to take big shots to score big goals," I mutter. I set my coffee down. "But it really is a metaphor for me...like I always felt like the stuff I was doing was all for a bigger purpose. Really I guess I was just hogging the ball."

Chloe stretches her arms over her head and twists, cracking her back. "I still think you would have made a really good sweeper, Teddy. You do have a great vision and you do form terrific strategies."

I'm about to remind her I'm no good at defense, but my phone rings. "It's Sara."

Chloe gestures for me to pick it up, so I do.

"You want to see that house? Are you still nearby? I'm five minutes away and I've got the key code."

32

CHLOE

5 WEEKS Later

I have no idea why I said yes to a closing date on the same day another round of revisions is due back to my editor. Communicating my wants and needs is obviously still a work in progress for me, but Teddy and I are really starting to enjoy our time with Pam. Sometimes we even see her separately to talk through issues specific to each of us.

Regardless, I'm rushing around gathering up papers as Teddy paces the hall. We've both been staying here at the Highland Park house, but we're living out of boxes and our things are heaped everywhere.

He's trying to work remotely today and I hear him on the phone with his assistant. I've noticed his work voice has changed over the past few weeks. His tone is calmer and I think he's using his marriage counseling strategies with his colleagues. I should ask him about it.

"Later," I mutter, scooping up the last handful of printed pages I have scattered across my desk. I back up, intending to move them into my bag, when I trip over the dog.

I fall to my butt in a cloud of yelping fur and fluttering

paper. Teddy pokes his head in the office door and says, "José, I gotta call you back...yep. See if that time works out for Yvonne. Thanks."

He crouches beside me. "You all right?" I can't tell if he's talking to me or the dog. I groan, seeing the pages all flung around out of order.

Teddy starts to stack the pages and I'm grateful as I see him slowly sorting them in numerical order. "What's this mean?" He points to the bold, red type taking up most of a page. "TK?"

I nod. "TK is short for 'to come.' Like, that's the part I'm still working on. Still in progress."

He squints at the page and then looks at me. "This is a spicy part!"

I nod, grinning. "Yeah. I didn't have it in me to write that scene when it was due, but I didn't want to hold up the editing process." I shrug. "I can add it in later."

"You TK'd the best part." He shakes his head as he straightens up the stack of pages.

I smile, reaching for them. "The best part is still to come."

Teddy pauses, scooping up the dog and kissing the top of his furry head. "I like that, Chloe. The best part is TK."

We both look at the dog and he wags his tail, tongue poking out as he pants excitedly. "TK?" Teddy tilts his head and says it again. "Is that your name, buddy? Are you T.K.?"

He barks, a definitive yelp. I laugh. "I guess we finally named the dog."

Teddy stands up and offers me a hand, tugging me to my feet. "Now let's go get him a yard."

.   .   .

SARA GREETS us at her office with stress balls and a smile. "You'll want to squeeze these periodically between signatures. It'll keep you from getting a sore wrist."

We are closing on the sale of the McMansion and the purchase of the Craftsman at the same time. Teddy stares at his ball quizzically, but I squeeze the foam in excitement, eager to move into this new phase of our lives. It takes us under an hour to sign all ten thousand documents and soon, Teddy and are standing on our new driveway with T.K.

"You have the keys?" Teddy seems as excited as me, bouncing in his shoes and fiddling with T.K.'s leash. I nod, looking between the house and the office. I bite my lip, unable to decide which I want to open first.

"Stay right there," Teddy says, pointing and handing me the leash. He quickly sprints to the car and pulls a gift bag from the back seat. "I got you something."

He beckons for the leash and trades me, handing me the silver bag. I'm surprised by its weight and I flush, touched by him giving me an unexpected gift. "I didn't get you anything, Bear."

He smiles. "Every day with you is a gift, my love."

I roll my eyes, groaning as he continues to recite lines from my second book. "I guess you're getting caught up with Chloe Petals."

"I am indeed." He waggles his eyebrows. "Open your gift, babe."

I reach into the bag and pull out a sturdy metal plate and I gasp when I see what it says. Teddy got me an oil-rubbed bronze plaque with SCANDAL SHEET PRESS HEADQUARTERS in raised letters.

When I look up at my husband, I see he's got the dog situated in the fenced-in yard and Teddy is leaning on the front door to the office space, the sunlight filtering through the slats of the pergola above his head. "Shall we explore your HQ, madam?"

I nod and dig the keys back out of my pocket, tears of joy brimming in my eyes. We walk inside the room and I spin around, imagining where I'll put my desk, where I'll install shelves, and where I'll host Foof events if we ever need to meet when Bridges and Bitters is closed. I clap my hands and squeal. "This is it," I whisper.

I rush over to Teddy and kiss him and he wraps me tightly in his arms, picking me up and spinning me a few times. He sets me back down and presses his forehead against mine. "The best part is TK," he whispers.

"Definitely." I kiss him again and we walk toward the main house, holding hands.

EPILOGUE: TEDDY
ONE YEAR LATER

"YOU SURE YOU don't want me to go in with you?" Chloe fidgets with her purse in the hall of the fertility clinic.

I shake my head. "I think that would make it even weirder."

She nods. "Okay, then. Fist bump for luck?" I tap her knuckles with mine, but not very enthusiastically. "Have fun with *Busty Office Babes.*" Chloe laughs nervously. "Do you think they changed out the video?"

"I have no idea. I'm not going to watch it." I check my pocket for the specimen cup and sigh. When I look at Chloe again, she's smirking.

"Check your phone. Wait. Do you have service in here?"

We both look at my phone and see that I do not, in fact, have service deep inside the hospital. I try to connect to the free wi-fi and check the box that I understand I won't be able to visit websites with inappropriate content. "They really don't make it easy for guys to produce a specimen," I mutter. A text comes through, from Chloe. "Is this what you wanted me to see?"

She nods and points to the door. "It's for in there. I'll see you in two hours." She stretches up to kiss my cheek and heads down the hall.

I walk into PRIVATE ROOM A and try to decide if I'm going to sit on the couch that's been bleached so many times the vinyl cushions are faded. I decide to stand in the center of the room and drop my pants. I set the collection cup on the table, where a laminated sign reminds me again that I can't use lube or it'll contaminate the sample.

I sigh and fist my junk, pulling up the text from Chloe. I hope it's not another article about sperm wash techniques. I almost drop the phone when I see that it's a document Chloe wrote herself.

Third Time's the Charm, by Chloe Preston

"Preston, huh?" I swallow and decide I'll turn the lights off in the room. It'll go easier if it seems like it's just me and my phone and a love note from my wife.

I'd been wet for him for hours, soaking through the leggings I wore just to tempt him. I wonder if he thought of me at home all day, with no panties, as he sat behind his desk.

"Holy shit." I actually do drop the phone when I realize what Chloe has done here. I fumble around on the floor and find my phone. I decide to sit on the tile and use the glow from the screen to grab the cup so it's nearby. My dick is much more responsive now and I give it a firm squeeze in appreciation.

Teddy walked in the door to find me spread out on the couch, one hand down the front of my pants, lazily toying with my clit as I waited for him. He dropped his briefcase and his jaw as he realized what I was doing.

I shake myself free of the fantasy and recognize this story as something that Chloe actually did a few weeks ago.

I groan and then gasp, not wanting to make noise in here. I'm so turned on, reading her interpretation of what we did together, of how I fucked her on the couch, then over the back of the couch while I pulled her hair. She details all of it here for me, only the way she words everything makes it sound so much sexier than my memory.

As he pounded into me, I felt the earth move—but maybe it was just that solid presence, reminding me that I am his. That he is mine, mine, mine. He grunted as he slammed into me, and I knew I'd feel this the next day as I sat and tried to work.

My hand flies over my cock as I read and remember the look of Chloe, splayed open for me, body swallowing my length. She was so wet that day it spread down her thighs and my dick glistened with her arousal as it moved in and out of her.

"God, yes, fuck me, Teddy," I wailed, my face muffled by the cushions of the couch. He drove my hips into the frame until I worried it would break. And then I didn't care as I came so hard my teeth rattled. Teddy swelled inside me and then I felt him coming, felt the hot spurts as he—

I toss the phone and grab the sample cup, making sure I'm lined up inside the rim as I finish. By the time I'm done, I'm shaking and breathing hard. I feel an intense wave of gratitude that my wife was able to help me forget where I was, that I was able to dive inside her story of us. I'll have to finish reading it later.

I clear my throat and stand up, careful to keep the cup upright as I feel around for the light switch. I wash my hands and get myself wiped off and tucked in before I head down the hall to turn in the specimen cup.

I try to kill time in the cafeteria while I wait for go-time, but I can't concentrate. Between the anticipation of maybe making a baby today and the knowledge that my wife found a way to insert herself into my portion of the procedure, my mind is like microwave popcorn.

When I finally make my way to the exam room to find Chloe, I blush at the sight of her. She's wearing a paper gown and a smug expression. I check to make sure we're alone in the room before I kiss her. "You're a naughty woman."

She bites my lip and laughs, lacing her fingers together behind her head. "I can't wait to hear what you thought of my latest publication."

I sink into the squeaky chair by her head. "You know what I thought of it. I thought very highly of it, Mrs. Preston."

She rolls onto her side and reaches for my hand, which I squeeze. Dr. McClendon raps on the door and pokes her head in, smiling. "Who's ready to make a baby?"

I hear Chloe inhale sharply and I drape an arm around her shoulders as I continue to hold her hand. This feels a lot different from the first time we tried to conceive. But I know this is the best option for us for this moment, and it feels good knowing how hard we worked to get here together.

Dr. M, as she asks us to call her, narrates as she works, sliding the tube inside Chloe and preparing. "I've got a half milliliter of perfect sperm here, Preston family." She grins. "I've got a great feeling about this."

I lean closer to Chloe and look into her eyes. I drop a kiss on her forehead and we both squeeze our hands. I whisper into her ear, my lips brushing against her beautiful hair. "I've got a great feeling, too."

. . .

THANK YOU FOR READING! **The Bridges and Bitters series continues with Speed Rail: A Single Dad Romance starring Piper and the neighbor she thinks she can't stand.**

Want to see what happens next for Chloe and Teddy? Click here for a steamy bonus epilogue.

Eager for more Foof fun? We first meet these ladies in Vibration: An Accidental Roommates Romance .

AUTHOR'S NOTE

I first learned that marriage-in-crisis romance was *a thing* when I picked up Lyssa Kay Adams' Bromance Book Club early in pandemic. The trope appealed to me immediately, as I was quarantined at home with my husband and three sons and two rescued rabbits.

I decided mid-way through writing my Brady Family series that I would someday write a marriage-in-crisis romance, and I began reading every book in that trope I could get my hands on. There aren't too many, as it turns out!

I knew from the start that Chloe and Teddy would be my couple in crisis, and I knew infertility would be the catalyst for their crisis. I began asking my friends all about infertility, and realized I had an in with a fertility research clinic here in Pittsburgh.

What an adventure! The scientists there all think their work is monotonous, and I think it's magical. I stood with my note pad, peering into drawers and freezers and heaters overflowing with vats of sperm. I asked questions for an hour straight.

And then, like Jamie Fraser in
look at sperm under a microscope
help me see the debris around tha
all looked the same to my untrain
to read a draft of this book to ma
stuff right.

I then interviewed people wh
tility and who attempted the sam
and Chloe. People casually joke
baking their balls and reminisced
in the videos in the sample collec
they conveyed the strain of that t
thankful for the time and energy
their experiences and I hope I did t

As for Chloe's work writing he
related to pandemic, too. Quarant
old house with my husband and so
obsessed with who might have qu
the 1918 Spanish Flu Pandemic. I
history for myself, because that ex
house historian out for coffee and
work.

I found another historical resea
the archives downtown. I spent th
old books the size of me, imagin
digging up dirty secrets and re-imag

That's a very long-winded ove
came to life. I hope you enjoyed it.
for Teddy and Chloe. I always kno
back together in the end.

~Lainey

www.ingramcontent.com/pod-product-compliance
Lightning Source LLC
Chambersburg PA
CBHW030827020726
47499CB00006B/2097

9 781957 145211